T0193251

BIKINI
BRAVO

BOOK TWO IN THE ARGUS SERIES

BIKINI BRAVO

Maskirovka
Are you ready for the truth?

WILLY MITCHELL

BIKINI BRAVO
MASKIROVKA

iUniverse books may be ordered through booksellers or by contacting:

iUniverse
1663 Liberty Drive
Bloomington, IN 47403
www.iuniverse.com
1-800-Authors (1-800-288-4677)

ISBN: 978-1-5320-8873-5 (sc)
ISBN: 978-1-5320-8874-2 (hc)
ISBN: 978-1-5320-8872-8 (e)

Library of Congress Control Number: 2019918696

Print information available on the last page.

iUniverse rev. date: 11/21/2019

For those soldiers who manage to lead lives beyond the atrocities. For those loved ones who cope with the trauma of life, war, poverty, sickness, and homelessness.

We are the Pilgrims, master; we shall go
Always a little further: it may be
Beyond the last blue mountain barred with snow,
Across the angry or that glimmering sea,
White on a throne or guarded in a cave
There lives a prophet who can understand
Why men were born: but surely, we are brave,
Who make the Golden Journey to Samarkand.

—James Elroy Flecker, "The Golden
Journey to Samarkand"

CONTENTS

Part IV Fuck You

Part V Flip Side

ACKNOWLEDGMENTS

THANK YOU TO MY AMAZING wife and wonderful daughter for all your patience, support, and—above all—love.

Bikini Bravo is the second book in the Argus series, following *Operation Argus*. Thanks to all those whose stories inspired these books, including everyone who has sacrificed for liberty, freedom, good, and right.

Although *Bikini Bravo* is a novel, it is based on actual events. In most cases, the names have been changed to protect the innocent, the dirty, the rotten, the good, and the pure.

You know who you are!

WWW.WILLYMITCHELL.COM

AUTHOR'S NOTE

AS A MAN OF THE world, I've heard many tales from all kinds of people ... the sober, drunk, delusional, disillusioned, dreamers, schemers, and downright believers. These tales inform me both as a person and as an author, and they blend reality into fiction in the pages to come as we embark on the second novel in the Argus series.

For example, I've heard tales of Central American grandmothers pimping out their granddaughters while nursing their great-grandchildren in their arms. About a Brazilian *girl of the night* in Sydney who unexpectedly encountered her uncle, and how the man bedded her just the same. Or tales of unspeakable genocide, religious persecution, and terrorism. Human beings seem to be willing to do just about anything to themselves and to one another.

We've all witnessed how human suffering plays out on the nightly news. Yet we often turn a blind eye when it suits us in our busy lives. Ironically, when oil and riches play a part in the story, then people pay more attention because the impact could hit closer to home. Corrupt governments, the dark web, geopolitics, world economics, climate change ...

the list goes on and on. At times, it's hard to know what to believe. Life is often stranger than fiction.

And therein lies the beauty of the Argus series of thrillers. Based on the exploits of a group of former veterans of an elite branch of the British Army, 22 Special Air Service, the novels provide a glimpse into the way these types of units operate and how the men and women within them interact on a personal and professional basis. The reader may ask, "Is this fact? Or is this fiction?" Truth be told, the stories are a blend of reality and imagination. In the pages to come, you'll find plenty of references to real-world events, people, and places. The present times create an intriguing background for the plot.

The first novel in the series was *Operation Argus*, a stirring tale of courage, intrigue, and treachery that involved Mitch as the hero as he and the crew uncovered a sinister Russian plot that involved the murder of their best friend. In *Bikini Bravo*, Russian villain Dimitri Dankov seeks revenge on the group, particularly Mitch, after an assassination attempt fails. As Bella, Mitch's daughter and the protagonist of *Bikini Bravo*, works with the group, they discover that the world's leading drug cartels have partnered with Russia to take over Equatorial Guinea. Plenty of action ensues as the plot speeds to a dramatic and tragic end readers won't see coming.

Before we get started, there are three words that require explanation.

Bikini: The Bikini state was an alert state indicator previously used by the UK Ministry of Defence to warn of nonspecific forms of threat, including civil disorder, terrorism, or war. The levels of risk went up in a series of risk from White to Black, Black Special, Amber, and Red being the highest state of alert.

Bravo: Part of the NATO phonetic alphabet assigned codewords acrophonically to the letters of the English alphabet. The twenty-six code words in the NATO phonetic alphabet are assigned to the twenty-six letters of the English alphabet in alphabetical order as follows: Alpha, Bravo, Charlie, Delta, Echo, Foxtrot, Golf, Hotel, India, Juliet, Kilo, Lima, Mike, November, Oscar, Papa, Quebec, Romeo, Sierra, Tango, Uniform, Victor, Whisky, X-ray, Yankee, Zulu.

Maskirovka: *maːskɪ'rɒvkə*//*ˌmaskɪ'rɒvkə*/ noun: In Russia and other countries of the former Soviet Union: political or military deception, especially as practiced against Western intelligence. Origin: 1970s. From Russian *maskirovka*—masking, disguise, camouflage; from *maskirovat'*—to mask, disguise, camouflage (from French *masquer*).

PROLOGUE

December 2003
Malindi, Kenya, East Africa
6:00 p.m.

I TOOK A WALK AROUND the town and in hindsight had ventured too far into the native market for a white man, realizing that I was now the only Westerner in sight. The market became narrower, more congested. I became more and more an unwanted source of distraction. The heat and humidity of the day were lingering as nightfall came. The market vendors lit their stoves and boiled their kettles and made their potions. The rancid smell of stagnant, mosquito-infested water and street latrines permeated the air.

As I walked, I was tracked by bright, staring, big white eyes popping out of the growing darkness like fireflies in the night. The armless, the legless, the blind, and the inflicted pleaded for money, cigarettes, or food, in that order. The lepers held out their feeble and gnarled hands for a coin or two, or a note—even better. A man with no legs was on a makeshift skateboard. I found it incomprehensible that apparently some of these beggars had self-inflicted injuries, and the more gruesome their injuries, the higher their value on the street.

I noticed a difference in Africa distinct from my other travels. It was their eyes, always an element of sadness behind them, trying to make a living, surviving from day to day. The scarcity of clean, drinkable water, the lack of food and nutrition, the near absence of health care, the void of money or opportunity for income, the despair, the loss of hope, the closest to base survival the human form can get. *Surely, they would be better off away from the cities and the towns, surviving in nature, harvesting the natural resources that exist*, I thought. Then I reminded myself of the unforgiving sun, the raw, almost unbearable heat, the miles and miles between water holes, the hierarchy of the food chain, and of course the constant threat from hungry and persistent predators.

That night, the eyes turned from sadness to jealousy to envy and worse. The level of interest was uncomfortable as I picked up my pace and headed back to the main town.

I turned back, retraced my steps past the various street market vendors selling food—all either from local farms, probably these the farmers themselves—clothing, furniture, or handcrafted items, many of the street sellers hawking their wares in the market stalls behind.

A witch doctor with his crazed devil eyes, his feathers, his beads, and his bare feet was stamping the ground. He wore a loin cloth, a red robe, and the skin of some wild animal wrapped around his shoulders. His intricately carved pole was brandished above his head in time with the stamps of his feet as he wailed, hissed, and howled, his elephant scrotum full of the strangest mementos, ready to read someone's future if they so dared.

A mosquito buzzed around my ear. I slapped with my right hand, clapped my ear, and missed the mosquito, deafening myself for a few moments. I stared the witch doctor in the eye. It was a *fuck off and leave me alone* kind of stare. His powers of reading the mind must have worked. He left me alone.

Back to the main street and civilization—the deep red dirt below that had compacted over years, the *matatu* (bus) speeding through the town, and the driver bobbing around at the wheel, battling to keep it on the road without taking the foot off the pedal. Anyone in their way would get mowed down. Just the previous day, a local woman fell victim. No police, no incident report, no funeral, just her body left on the side of the road to get eaten by the ubiquitous vermin present in these parts of the world.

I felt relieved to escape the market, the witch doctor, and the matatu. With a silent glance at the Lord above, I stumbled into the bar.

What are you doing here, William Mitchell? I asked myself. *Why didn't I go to Blackpool or Benidorm or Ayia Napa or the Costa bloody Del Sol instead of this fucking shithole? At least I will be back in Glasgow for Christmas Day,* I thought as I contemplated the long trip back from Nairobi to London, then home the following morning. Back to my mobile fucking home and my Fray Bentos pie for fucking Christmas! *Still. Better than this shithole,* I thought.

I had come to supervise a pair of ships decommissioning in the unique East African style—full speed ahead, point it at the shore, and run it up the beach, and just like the woman's body on the side of the road, it would be stripped bare without a trace in a matter of days. Just like the bus driver and the local police, this method saved the ship owners a ton of money and paperwork.

That's Africa, baby, I reminded myself of the old saying. *TAB.*

I got myself a Heineken and took a seat at a table away from the bar, on the stoop overlooking the main street of Malindi. I was feeling cantankerous and wanted to be alone—often how I best liked it. I was okay with my own company. I had gotten used to it. I liked my company more and more and that of others less and less over the years.

I sat there for a while, relieved to be back in the relative safety of the bar, watching the Malindi world go by and this colorful mixture of characters.

The crowd was different—those who could afford the luxury of a beer. For many, it was a day or more in wages in this part of the world.

I looked down at my hands, all withered and worn now. Too many days on the tools in the shipyards and on the *Clyde.* I was now running a shift, a union supervisor. I hated the job nowadays, the bureaucracy. How things had changed from the old days. Making a run to Kenya was a welcome respite.

An eclectic mix populated the bar—from a couple of colonials in their old-as-time linen suits to neighbors from Ethiopia and Somalia with their distinctly colorful robes and headgear, to those from farther afield, Egypt with their fezzes, Indonesia, and India, with a different style of robe but nonetheless colorful. And then, one by one, in walked a different group. White in skin, rugged in nature, and by their gaits and demeanor, a very interesting group—mostly ex-military I guessed.

The place was busy. The unusual group sat close to me, carefully looking me up and down, trying to figure me out. I kept quiet, investigated my glass, and realized that I was close enough to listen, to catch the odd word muttered. I had heard enough stories in my past to piece it together and get the gist of the situation and their conversation.

The leader of the group was a tall, big man with a mop of white-blond hair. The product of Harrow or Eton, I guessed, versus some of the more pedestrian and cheaper options in well-heeled London and surrounding areas. The others were of a different breed. Blondie, it seemed, was the ideas man, and the others were the soldiers. *A colonel with his troops*, I thought.

As I started my second Heineken and their introductory conversations subsided, the nitty-gritty of their conversation piqued my interest—corruption, oil, West Africa, coup.

In walked Silver Fox.

If Blondie was the colonel, then Silver Fox was the general and was very clearly in charge, as he commanded immediate attention from his audience. Smart suit, uncrumpled despite the humidity, gray hair, and piercing gray eyes. Pearson was his name apparently, and he had the insights that the others seemingly needed to hear. Resources, people, connections, and timing, all designed to overthrow some tin-pot government in some highly corrupt nation in Africa, which didn't really narrow it down too much.

Reference to large oil reserves and a potential pot of black gold helped but with no conclusive answer.

Looking at this collection of men gathered, it was clear that they were up to no good. My guess was that that there was a big prize at stake and that this was clearly a profession, not just a job for these men.

After thirty minutes, Blondie and Silver Fox paused for a short debrief and then disappeared in opposite directions as quickly as they had arrived. The remainder of the group sat and mulled over what they had just heard, almost looking in shock.

Later that evening as I sat sipping on my second double Glenfarclas, a group of three Maasai warriors, complete with ox-blood plaits, red robes, and their assegais, approached the group of men to sell their wares. The biggest of the mercenary group simply looked the leader of the three Maasai in the eye and uttered, "Fuck off," in a way that was obvious in any language to move on and get out of the way. The three Maasai did just that.

These mercenary men had a presence about them, a level of intimidation and purpose. I sensed that they were used to violence, and those in their presence could be subjected to that at any moment. For most, the company of men like this was uncomfortable, like a single gazelle in the company of a pride of lions. They created that level of apprehension without effort. It was just who they were.

As the night wore on and their beers turned into whisky, the men mellowed, and then one by one, they left the bar into the hot, steamy Kenyan night.

A few months later, back home in Glasgow, on the BBC Scotland News, I saw the photo of Blondie on the screen and then the same men from the bar in Malindi. It was them. A photo of a former prime minister's son, a high-ranking diplomat of sorts, funding from unknown sources, and a group of former special services mercenaries caught, armed to the teeth, heading to a remote land, Equatorial Guinea, Africa's sixth-largest oil-rich nation. My mind raced.

This operation was apparently called the Wonga Coup, and fifteen years later, the same principles of the attempted coup in Equatorial Guinea would be applied again but by an extraordinary coalition and group of collaborators.

This is the story of how a group of greedy oil executives, a Mexican drug cartel, and the state-backed Russian Mafia affected a coup for power over that oil-rich African nation.

This is the story of Bikini Bravo.

PART I

THE BEGINNING

I

BIKINI BRAVO

January 2004
Amenas, Algeria
2:30 a.m.

BIG BAD BOB WIPED THE sweat from his forehead with the back side of his right hand and peered out the open side door of the AS365 Dauphin, a fast chopper with plenty of guns to take down any bad guys who might show up. He was pretty sure his crew would be landing in a hot zone, as would the crew aboard the other chopper flying in close formation right next to his aircraft. The night was still. No light pollution, apart from the stars, when passing by the occasional town as they skirted wide to avoid any detection on their 180-mile journey down the Algerian side of the Libyan border from their origin just across the southern border of Tunisia.

Bob considered the action to come with the cool head of an experienced combat soldier. He and the fifteen other special ops guys with him from the Special Air Service, an elite British Army strike force, passed over a couple of groups of herders on their way down the border. The down thrust of the Dauphins blew up the dust, bothered their herds, and blew the Bedouin tents. They were gone as quickly as they had come and, at that time of the morning, left a memory of what could easily be thought of as a dream or a mystic wind.

As they neared In Amenas and their target, the crews got ready to engage—balaclavas on, gas masks on, night vision on, magazine in, cocked, safety. The crew had rehearsed this type of mission several times over in the Brecon Beacons, Anglesey, in Scotland and during operations in Northern Ireland. The men of call sign Bikini Bravo had been fully briefed on the target building and its occupants—the outer walls of the compound, the single entrance, the courtyard within, the rooftop, the living quarters, the sleeping quarters.

The pair of Dauphins swung south of the desert town, keeping wide and low as they swept around to the location of the compound. Bob sat in silence with only the voice of the pilots in his earpiece, talking to him and the rest of the crew through their approach. In moments, they would be hovering over the compound, making their way on to the rooftop and their operation for that night.

As the pilot hovered and lowered, a new but familiar voice could be heard. "Green, green, green. Go, go, go."

The two AS365s hovered above the rooftop of the compound, with the down thrust of the chopper blades swaying the ornamental plants like a hurricane had descended upon them. Bob and his men spilled out of the black helicopters on to the rooftop like a group of worker bees and quickly made their way, clearly planned, into the house below, going about their predetermined, very deliberate, and deathly tasks.

The boy gazed up at the canopy of stars illuminating the desert sky as he shone a flashlight on the star chart one of his uncles had given him. He had long been fascinated with stargazing, and he liked the challenge of identifying the various constellations. At age fifteen, he knew he was smarter than most of his peers, and as he studied the heavens, he felt a keen sense of satisfaction at being outside the compound on such a beautiful evening. He was just outside the zone of the orange security lights, allowing him to be practically invisible if any of the security detail happened to come along. Yes, he was outside and alone. Blissfully alone. Life in the compound with his influential father was like living in a fishbowl. He hated it. He was always under the watchful eye of the security guards. He'd been locked up with his reclusive family for far too long. He had no friends. He couldn't. Interacting with the local population was strictly forbidden.

What's that? he wondered as he looked in the direction of the sound. He'd heard that sound before, the *thump, thump, thump* of helicopter rotors. He got to his feet as two choppers came in right over him. Scarcely believing his eyes, he watched in horror as heavily armed soldiers dressed in black began to rappel down to the roof of the compound.

Within ninety seconds, spurts of gunfire spat into the desert night from different parts of the compound. He could only imagine what was occurring. Shaking his head was the only movement he could muster. He was terrified, paralyzed with fear. He could feel the warm sensation of his urine as he lost control of his bodily functions in the trauma of it all.

He watched two of the men return and manhandle what he assumed was a body bag into one of the helicopters, and the remainder of the teams made their way back up to the rooftop from wherever they had just been.

The boy could clearly see the leader in the dim light. He was a big man, standing around six foot three. He pulled off his balaclava and gas mask, ushering the teams back on to their rides home. The boy could see the leader looking around the rooftop, taking one last sweep of the scene before jumping aboard. The door closed behind him, and they disappeared into the night.

The boy lived with his father, mother, and sister. It was a strange kind of existence even for a family who lived on the edge of the desert and close to the fractious border with Libya.

His father was a very proud man and deeply religious. It seemed that he was revered and had a steady stream of visitors from many parts of the world, often bearing gifts.

He had his own security guards that kept enemies outside of the four walls, but the boy did not know who these enemies were. He concluded that his father was considered important, as the visitors who came were always very polite and deeply respectful in his company.

He knew that his father despised the West, and even sleeping under the stars with his map of the skies would aggravate him, but the boy didn't care. He wanted to break out, go to a normal school. He wanted to play football with the other kids that he could see from the rooftop. He wanted to wear Western clothes and not his robes. He wanted to be normal, but he suspected that it might never be the case.

He had not been outside of the compound in nearly two years.

That night, after they had gone, he slowly walked through the house, frightened, finding dead bodies in almost every room. His father's bodyguards, dead. The house staff, dead. His tutor, dead. He went to his mother's bedroom and found her dead too, with a single bullet wound in her forehead. His sister, only eight years old, dead in her arms.

Sobbing uncontrollably, he went back to the rooftop where he had seen the helicopters and the men in black. He saw the face of the man, their leader. After all, he was now free from the things that held him so dear. His family was gone. He would never forget that night. Nor would he ever forget that face.

TCC International News: Deputy Head of Al Qaeda Dead

London, Breaking News: Tonight, we are getting reports that a small group of elite special forces personnel have successfully eliminated the number two in the Al Qaeda group, Mohammed Hamza, and second in command to the world's most wanted man, Osama Bin Laden.

The raid took place in the early hours of this morning on the border between Algeria and Libya, two hundred miles south of the Tunisian border.

Hamza's body was taken back to HMS *Fearless*, and an at-sea burial was completed after the raid.

2
BOOTCAMP

May 2017
Camp Peary, The Farm
Williamsburg, Virginia, United States
2:00 p.m.

BELLA HAD DECIDED OVER CHRISTMAS break, in consultation with her father, to go straight for the Central Intelligence Agency as her career of choice. She realized after the debacle with Nikita, a best male friend of hers who had gotten himself involved with some really bad guys in the international banking business, that her role as a risk analyst with Executive Outcomes simply wouldn't cut it anymore. Instead, the idea of following in her father's footsteps in the intelligence game drew her to the CIA. The shift from executive to spook was downright attractive. Plus, being somewhat of an idealist, she wanted to make a positive difference in the world.

After she was dropped off at the gates of Camp Peary, she walked up to the checkpoint surrounded on either side by wire fencing and barbed wire on top, marking the entrance to this mysterious nine-thousand-acre training facility of the Central Intelligence Agency and clandestine operations, built in 1942.

She remembered her father's stories of his first days arriving at Stirling Lines, then headquarters of Twenty-Second Special Air Service in Hereford, England, and his descriptions resonated as she approached. *Just bigger and more profound*, she thought as the simple, understated sign ahead loomed, Camp Peary. Behind it was the green-roofed, redbrick building that was the checkpoint and her gateway to her home for the next few months.

When she was a teenager, Mitch would take Bella to the shooting range in San Rafael, familiarizing her with the safety issues around gun handling, then getting comfortable with the weapon as an extension of the body.

Safety and level of confidence were the basis of expertise, and then the art of hitting the target where you want, when you want, with the greatest of instinctive accuracy and impact.

Mitch had explained to her that the New Zealand All Blacks started playing rugby when they were all but out of their prams; the same with Brazilians and football, Canadians and ice hockey, and marksmen with rifles and guns.

The final stage was moving on from Mitch's weapon of choice, the 9 mm Browning Hi Power to more exotic 9 mm options—Sig Sauer, Glock, Berretta, Walther—then on beyond 9 mm.

She remembered the first time she had fired the Magnum Desert Eagle and the sheer power of that beast. She reflected and realized that, without the previous steps of safety and confidence, she probably would not have handled the flash, the noise, and the sheer recoil of the thing.

She also recalled Mitch's boxing club down in the Mission District, San Francisco, and similarly how he had taught her the basics of the stance, the defense, and then the different punches as she would work on the bags in the gym, practicing her sequences. She learned these skills without ever using them. Mitch told Bella that he regarded her as too young, beautiful, and precious to use them for real. It did, however, advance her sparring bouts with the boxing pros at the club, who just stood back and helped her get the sense of the fight.

It was this training and these skills that had helped her in her chosen career. She was a natural on the range. She knew almost every weapon, and even with the ones that she didn't, her pick-up was good. Second nature. She knew how to defend and attack, but most of all, Mitch had taught her the art of assessment—interpreting circumstances quickly and taking decisive and immediate action.

She remembered in Argus when Nikita had to get back to London and how she had evaded her suitors in their crumpled suits and taken Nikita's 5.0-liter, supercharged, F-Type Jaguar XKR from the Pisa airstrip, over the alps, and back to Blighty. Mitch had even taught her the rules of evasive and pursuit driving.

As she entered the gates of the legendry but secret training facility, she knew that she had a lot to thank Mitch for and realized that, for her entire life to this point, she had been in training. She just hadn't known it at the time.

She passed through the checkpoint, and a vehicle with a friendly driver chauffeured her through the property to join her cohort. She noticed the irony of the boat shed as they passed by and thought of her father, her hero, Mitch, once again. With his presence, she knew that she could do it. He gave her the confidence but also the challenge. He always taught her *who dares wins* and of course the motto of the Special Air Service, Stirling Lines, and where the legendary, mystical, and nonexistent Boat Shed originated.

"For all those that have passed here before, I will honor you and join your ranks. I will tread where others have tried and failed. I will give it my all and cease at nothing but to survive and succeed."

Bella uttered the words under her breath, words that she had learned as a young girl, learning from the teachings of her father, "Forward."

She looked out the window as they pulled up to a single-story, redbrick building with another understated sign: Training Headquarters, Welcome.

Bella was used to understated. She got it. To be successful in this future career, being understated was a requirement. Not standing out from the crowd, keeping a low profile, not drawing too much attention to yourself. She recalled her father and his friends, and despite being some of the most fearsome men on the planet, they looked like a collection of rugby teammates, coworkers from the local construction company, a normal-looking group of men. They were like their pursuit cars, not Ferraris or with go-faster stripes and fancy alloy wheels; they were seemingly normal on the outside but supercharged within.

Time passed. Bella's rigorous training kept her so focused that she scarcely noticed how the days lapsed into weeks. And then she was finished with her preliminary courses and was shocked to discover that she'd ended up finishing top of her class at Camp Peary, in everything, literally. Not just the physical things but her understanding and comprehension of international politics, history, and the psychology of the world, helped of course by her stint at Executive Outcomes, where she had been a rising star for almost two years, and her lifelong apprenticeship under the instruction of her father, Mitch.

3

ARGUS

December 2016
Metelitsa Casino
Moscow, Russia
2:00 p.m.

DMITRI DANKOV AND HIS LAST remaining chief operation officer of sorts, Uri Bokov, arrived at the front of the casino in the black Mercedes S65. Dankov reflected how it had been a torrid few months for both men and their organization. Although their election play had proven successful with their man getting into the White House, another big successful bet through the First World Bank, there had been a lot of collateral damage, no less than their third lieutenant, Viktoria Saparov, the Black Widow, as she had otherwise been known.

Viktoria had disappeared off the face of the earth. Their team just outside of Vilnius, Lithuania, had been all but taken out. They were forced to temporarily close their casino operations and cashflow and now were retreating to the motherland until the heat subsided.

In the car on the way to the Metelitsa, they had sat in silence, watching the Moscow streets go by, reflecting on their meeting with the man in the Kremlin earlier that day, in its long, wide, marble corridors and the big door that opened to his office. Always smiles, it was never obvious what was going on in his mind. Still friends of the motherland, they both hoped, but one just never quite knew for certain, Dankov mused. Those were the stakes they played, that was their game, and this was the way they had chosen. Or, he often wondered, did it choose him?

The driver pulled in at the front of the casino, the VIP drop-off. It was a miserable, cloudy day in Moscow with the harsh Siberian winds passing through. The Metilitsa, like an expensive gold watch on a cheap suit, was bright, loud, garish, and without taste, but this was Russia, and this was one of their flagship casino operations in Moscow.

The two men got out of the car, assisted by the casino valet, and rushed from the cold outside into the warmth of the casino. Dankov put his arm around Bokov. "Davay vyp'yem, moy drug." (Let's go for a drink, my friend.) Of course, Dankov knew they weren't actually friends at all. Bokov ran Dankov's Asia operations. He was big, overweight, and sweaty and had an unhealthy addiction to sex. Man, woman, or boy didn't matter to him; therefore, Bangkok was a perfect location. Dankov tolerated him. In fact, he detested him, but he was necessary and was well connected in Asia, with his tentacles established in that part of the world. He was somewhat irreplaceable and had escaped Dankov's patience wearing thin, at least so far.

Once inside, they were ushered as VIP guests to the private suite next to the high stakes tables. Black carpet, black marble. Despite it being only two o'clock in the afternoon, it had no natural light but LED lighting to give the feel of an eighties' nightclub.

They were escorted to their table by two girls young enough to be their daughters, leaving not much to the imagination in terms of their clothing, or lack of it. They sat down, the distinctive gold, square bottle of Russo-Baltique vodka before them, with a bucket of ice and two glasses. One of the young ladies poured two generous measures. The men looked each other in the eye and raised their glasses. "Na Zdorovie!" They clashed the glasses and drank the clear spirit as if it were water. Dankov went to pour a top up. They deserved a good drink, he thought as he gave a big, bearlike smile to Bokov.

Bokov returned the smile, downed his vodka, and wiped his lips with the sleeve of his suit. He ogled the girls with undisguised lust. "Dimitri, my friend," he said, "I feel the urges coming on again. If you'll excuse me."

Dankov watched as Bokov got up from the table and hurried to the back of the casino. There was more than gambling going on, and Bokov clearly intended to avail himself of the opportunity to roll in the hay with some hapless young girl or boy.

Dankov returned his attention to the vodka and poured himself another shot. *Yes,* he thought, *Bokov is no Viktoria. That's for sure.*

15

The man didn't have her brains or her ruthless ambition. Although a loss to his organization, he appreciated her absence; always having to keep an extra eye out, she was always a threat of sorts.

Bokov was meant to be in Bangkok. That was where he belonged, Dankov thought as he now sipped more vodka and fell into his other thoughts.

It was true, the First World Bank project had been a huge success, generating billions of dollars and converting them into rubles for the motherland. Although temporarily off track, Dankov now had control of its assets through the Trakkai Investment Group Viktoria had created, and that would be his next move—step back from the dark operations for a while, take off the heat, and lay low.

His master plan was to use the First World Bank to help darker organizations legitimize their own dirty businesses, clean their dirty money, provide a safe haven, and of course for First World to leverage that huge amount of cash in investments and take a handsome profit off the top. It was a genius business idea, he thought as he raised the glass of vodka to himself in self-recognition.

Bokov returned from the private suite in the back with a big, greedy, dirty smile on his face, and that was the prompt for Dankov. "Satisfied? Come on, let's go." He ushered Bokov as they walked back the way they came to the S65 waiting for them out front. A couple of hours was enough respite for Dankov and frankly as much time as he could tolerate in the company of Bokov.

They both got in the back seat of the Mercedes, Bokov in the right, Dankov in the left. Dankov sat back into the premium leather as the Mercedes started to pull away. Almost with a sixth sense, he looked out the window. Across the road, he looked straight at Conrad Yee, 狗, Gǒu, the Dog, one of the world's deadliest assassins. Feeling the panic well up inside, Dankov tried to figure out why the Dog was standing across the street.

Oh my God, he thought in the split second before the bomb exploded.

PART II

ROOTS

4
WILD SIDE

February 2019
Langley, Virginia, United States
11:00 p.m.

THE THREE MEN CLOSELY FOLLOWED behind Bella, lurking in the dark shadows as she left the bar. Without turning her head to acknowledge their presence, she continued striding to her apartment. Rain started to come down in tiny spatters, just enough to moisten her face; in fact, it was quite refreshing and vitalizing under the circumstances.

Bella had been in the local bar after grabbing her singlet supper, and the three had tried to make a play. With her typical confidence, she had brushed them aside with her sharp wit and steely eye. They continued to try, and she continued to deny their efforts. They were clearly not her type with their baseball caps, tattoos, and gold teeth. She could almost smell the heroin on them and the bad news that oozed from their pores and personas.

As any professional in her line of business, she had weighed them up: the leader with his gold tooth, tattoos, and his sovereign bling; second in command with the silver duffel coat, big gold necklace on the outside of his black Nike shirt, pants hanging down, cheating gravity and below his hips, revealing a not-too-well-concealed pistol; and the third, the youngest by probably at least five years, the follower, nervousness in his soul. He was not the biggest problem of the three. She patted her chest and felt the comfort of her Glock 19 under her vest.

She waited around for closing in the hope that they would leave before her. It was obvious that they had some fixation, which made Bella uncomfortable but also alert and buzzed. She had felt this way before, and it made her uncomfortable in ways these three would never imagine.

Ever since she could remember, even as a toddler, her father had taught her well, not in the rough-and-tough sense but in the thinking sense. Mitch had taught her the lessons of a professional, thinking soldier, to plan, think through, think in advance about the outcomes, and execute. Like a chess player, she anticipated all her opponent's moves and game-ending possibilities in advance.

He had taught her the basics of field craft and communications, learning the signals for follow me, slow, stop, come to me, and quickly. They had a secret call that sounded like some nonexistent jungle bird, used to find each other in crowds, at night, or any time they were separated.

She was only six or seven when she visited Liddlesdale, Scotland, with her father, and as the day was growing old, they were giving up hope of finding the church and cemetery that Mitch and his own father had discovered in the same way decades earlier. Just as the sun was thinking about calling it a day above the beautiful, nowadays tranquil dale, with Hermitage Castle at its heart, they finally stumbled across the ancient church adorned with references to their clan and ancestors long past.

Bella remembered the graveyard, centuries old, the headstones weather-beaten and worn, barely readable carvings of names long past, not eerie but strangely comforting, being among family, just her, her father, and her clan.

The legend of her family and the teachings of history had been passed down from her father. A singer from the time she was a young child, the Scottish national anthem, "Flower of Scotland," was one of her first memorized songs. Her family had been brought down from the Highlands by Robert the Bruce to protect the Scottish border and gifted Hermitage Castle as the family seat. This once lawless region had been ruled by the Border Reivers, including her clan.

Her dad had taught her much, and as she kept an eye on the three men that she knew were going to cause trouble, she was once again grateful for his training. It provided the bedrock of her skill set, a skill set that had vaulted her into a rising-star position at the CIA. Her dad, a former career soldier, British Army, 22 Special Air Service, had been around a bit and had traversed the world to a laundry list of hot spots, ridding them of the bad guys and each time returning a little more serious than when he had left.

After leaving the Regiment, they moved to California, Marin County, where Bella's mum was originally from, and unlike the other kids at school whose fathers were policemen, firefighters, executives, or bankers, Mitch didn't return with gifts from Manhattan, Minneapolis, or Milwaukee but presents from far-off and mysterious lands. Growing up, she had been frustrated by his long periods of absence, lack of explanation of where he had been, and growing moods of self-isolation.

Bella knew she had a very special relationship with her father. They were connected more than by blood; they knew each other better than anyone else, almost telepathically. His teachings had been a great help to get her through Camp Peary and now in her current role with the CIA— International Affairs.

Business was booming. Bella was leveraging her previous experiences from the private start-up she joined straight from college, Executive Outcomes, never mind her experiences during Operation Argus—losing her godfather, Jimmy, and the closest thing she had found to a soul mate, Nikita, and his terrible and heartbreaking demise. She had moved on from that—well, sort of. Would she ever really forget?

She remembered the sight of Nikita dangling from his Hugo Boss belt in apartment 1b, Bromley High Street, and her extreme sadness and uncontrollable tears. She worked for twenty minutes trying to revive his still-warm body, but she was too late. Five minutes earlier, and she might have been able to save him.

Snap out of it, she thought, chastising herself for letting her mind wander in a situation that would surely go hot at any time.

"Hey, bitch, want to have some fun tonight?" the leader of the three shouted, his gold tooth catching the light of the streetlamp above.

Bella kept on walking, realizing that the three were now making ground on her.

"A little *party* with my friends and me?" Goldtooth persisted.

Bella was now buzzed. She had shirked off the temptation to just call 911 and dismissed the idea of deploying her Glock. As she arrived at the front gate of her apartment, the flagged path to the front door, she confirmed the plant pot she had carefully placed to the right of the door. She knew that when she breached the gate and the three behind her converged, the moment would be upon her.

Adrenalin rushing through her veins, her brain slowing the scene, her all-round peripheral vision down to a single frame per second, she didn't need to look; she knew the three were close. She could almost smell them.

As Bella got to her front door, she bent down to the plant pot, feigning to search for her keys. She could feel Goldtooth nearing when she grabbed an eighteen-inch monkey wrench she had stashed there just in case someone tried to jump her while she was unlocking the front door. In this case, she could've drawn down on them with the Glock 19, but she didn't want to actually kill anyone, and she knew she might if these guys got in her face. She hefted the cold steel in her hand. She straightened up with leopard-like swiftness as

Goldtooth reached out to grab her. She swung the wrench to the right side of his skull, looking her target deep in his eyes as she did so.

She saw the look of surprise, then confusion, then pain as the wrench connected with its full, blunt, and brutal force, sending Goldtooth to the ground, unconscious before he landed in a heap, like a sack of potatoes, by her doorstep.

Bella turned, and the second was upon her. With his silver duffel coat, gold chains around his neck, and backward baseball hat, he came at her with his sovereign rings shining in the light of the lamp by the side of the door, his fist heading toward her. Bella's instincts from her years of boxing kicked in. She moved her head and shoulders to one side, dipping her right shoulder and swinging the wrench to the side of his skull, connecting at the point his left ear joined his head, bursting and ripping his ear, leaving him squealing in pain. With her left fist, she attacked his right ear, disorientating him and adding to his pain. With her right foot, she kicked him hard in the solar plexus, sending him to the ground. A final blow to the head with the wrench sent him into unconsciousness. She stamped down on his right hand, hearing the bones crack, ending his ability to pick up, never mind use, the pistol she had spotted earlier in the bar, hidden in his pocket. She reached in, grabbed the pistol, and slid it in the waistband at the back of her pants for safekeeping.

The third, the youngest of the three, just stood there frozen, the shock plain on his face.

"Who the fuck are you, you crazy fucking lady?"

He started backing away slowly. "What the fuck did you just do?" he said in a high-pitched tone, like a kid in the schoolyard seeking to be heard by a teacher that might intervene and save him.

Bella stood there with the wrench in her right hand, staring back at the last remaining thug, left fist and jaw clenched tight, nose turned up and angry.

"No wonder someone wants you damaged, bitch. No wonder someone wants you fucking dead!"

That last remark interested Bella. She wondered what he meant, if anything, or if it was the drugs and alcohol talking. She smiled and shook her head as she watched him run away in utter terror.

"Afraid of a girl, are you?" she whispered. "Well, you should be afraid of this girl! Oh, yes you should, you fool."

Bella opened the front door, leaving the unconscious thugs bleeding on the sidewalk, and went inside. She tried to calm down, but the adrenaline rush was intense. Perhaps too intense.

Did I enjoy that a bit too much? she wondered.

She dialed a number in her CIA-issued phone, and just a few minutes later, police arrived with their flashing lights and Sig Sauer P226 pistols. Two uniformed cops got out of the cruiser. She recognized one of them, Officer Maloney, whom she'd met about two months earlier after having another dustup with some of the city's more unsavory critters.

"Fucking scumbags," Bella said as Maloney and his partner stopped in front of the two unconscious men bleeding on the sidewalk.

Officer Maloney whistled and shook his head. "Man, what'd you hit 'em with? A sledgehammer?"

Bella laughed. She liked this cop. He got straight to the point. "Something like that," she said.

"Jeez," he said, taking out his notebook. "You call 911? Or did your buddies at the Farm do it for you?"

Just then, a siren wailed in the distance. "They did. They've arranged to take care of this situation, but they wanted me to report it officially."

"Uh-huh," he said. "Then tell me what happened."

Bella did, with Maloney scribbling away in his notebook, grunting and uh-huhing as he did so.

"So, any injuries, miss? Cuts, bruises? Do you need to go to a hospital? See a nurse?" he asked, shaking his head as he asked.

Bella just stood there shaking her head, still breathing deeply with the adrenalin. Then she reached into her pants waistline, pulled out the P96, racked back the side to pop the round already in the chamber, switched the safety on, removed the magazine, and presented it to Maloney. "One of the them was carrying this."

"You don't see many of those in DC," commented Maloney.

Bella looked at the weapon and acknowledged the short, stubby, Russian-made 9 mm pistol.

As Bella finished explaining her evening, Maloney just said, "Is this your hobby or something? Why not take up yoga or flower arranging or needlework maybe?"

Bella just looked at him. "Of course, Officer. We women should just know our places, right?"

"That's not what I am saying here. What I am saying is that I have enough stuff to deal with, and twice maybe a coincidence, but if this thing turns into three times, well, that tells me there is more to this than meets the eye. Okay?"

Two ambulances arrived. After a short exchange between Maloney and the lead EMT, the EMTs hurried over to the downed men and began working on them.

"You think I like men attacking me on my doorstep, Maloney?"

"Obviously not. You're lucky they didn't get at you in a place you couldn't hold them off. You should be more careful."

"They asked for it; I didn't."

The ambulances drove away, their sirens off. Those men would get medical treatment but not at the local hospital. No, they'd wake up at the Farm for debriefing, or, more to the point, for interrogation. She'd mentioned on the CIA emergency call line that one of the men had been carrying a Russian-made handgun. That was enough to fan interest in the incident, even more than if it had just been an apparent sexual assault or mugging.

"We'll need you to come down to the station to give us your statement. I take it you're not going to press charges."

"No, I'm not."

The officers left, and Bella went inside. Several things bothered her as she slumped onto the sofa in the living room. The first was she seemed to enjoy fighting. The second was that the third man, the one who had run away, had hinted that there could possibly be a hit out on her.

Mitch had taught her well, maybe too well, over the years, between his boxing club on Mission Street, where he had taken her as a child, the various martial arts and different techniques, the stories, the teachings, and most importantly the self-disciplines associated with being ruthless in the theater of combat.

She had taken the saying *the eyes are the windows to the soul* a step further, and she could weigh up most situations through deep scrutiny, eye to eye, never yielding observation of her opponents' eyes. Mitch had often referred to this as clocking your enemy. Well, she'd clocked her enemies good, yet, as she sat in the dimly lit room, her mind teased over a number of things in her life that didn't seem quite right.

5

ALL QUIET

Waldorf Astoria
The Bund, Shanghai, People's Republic of China
10:00 p.m.

SITTING AT THE LONG BAR of what was formerly the colonial Shanghai Club, Mitch felt strangely at home in this country full of surprises and disappointments.

The trio of musicians found their way through various jazz renditions of once-popular tunes, translating them to barely recognizable versions of their past selves and presenting them in a pleasant enough way to accompany a whisky or two at the bar.

The pianist was a young girl from the Shanghai School of Music. The older African American guy hailed from Chicago and masterfully played various stringed instruments. The mesmerizing voice of the singer, apparently from Singapore, threaded it all together.

Mitch wasn't a great fan of China, but for the moment, he felt at home.

Mitch liked his own company, in fact, he preferred his own company, and that's just how it was tonight.

He had been asked to pop over for a week to help an old friend of Sam's do some consulting work—a security business based out of Shanghai, covering China and Southeast Asia. The Chinese were good at mimicking others' products, services, software, and hardware—everything from fake designer handbags and T-shirts to fake food. Everything from copied mobile phones to cars, computers, you name it. They were also trying to mimic Western security businesses, and that wasn't working out too well for them, at least so far.

As an air stewardess once shared with Mitch over a carton of Chinese apple juice, "In China, you never quite know what you are going to get, but always be prepared to be disappointed." She was right. "That's China," he told her at the time.

Sam was his old friend from the Regiment, former regimental sergeant major no less, now retired in Ross-on-Wye, tending his garden and his sheep on the small holding that he, his wife, Emily, and her parents had helped them to buy years before his meager army salary would have allowed.

Sam was still connected to the Regiment, an old favorite, although with each year that passed by, he knew fewer and fewer folks at their new state-of-the-art headquarters at Credenhill.

Since Emily had succumbed to breast cancer last year at the tender age of forty-eight, Sam had eventually started his book about his life as a soldier, his career with the Special Air Service, and his rise to the top noncommissioned job.

It was always hard to lose someone, no matter how often you have seen death. It was always more difficult when it was someone like Emily who didn't deserve to die, but who makes those decisions anyway? Sam would be okay. He was a leader, strong and levelheaded. The book he was writing would prove to be his savior, as would his immersion—following his father's footsteps in the education of young people, his flowerbeds, and his sheep.

Mitch's journey was a source of both pride and pain, from joining the British Army as a kid, his parents waving goodbye to him at the train station as he left with only his kit bag to basic training, then to the Blues and Royals, Ninth Parachute Squadron, Royal Engineers, Twenty-Ninth Commando, then to Hereford and 22 Special Air Service. It had been a good ride, like big Boy Scouts, as he often referred to his experiences and his time holding the queen's shilling.

He was a keen boxer in training and with the Blues and Royals, but rugby was his passion, and he had played for all of the regiments he served with, including in the Army Cup Final against 3 Para, and broke his ribs for the pleasure.

Mitch took his right hand and rubbed the ribs in question, as though reacting to the pain of his thoughts, but he did fondly remember the fun and the camaraderie of both rugby and the army.

The trio in the Long Bar announced that they were taking a break as half a dozen people lazily and half-heartedly clapped in a sort of feigned, polite appreciation. *Probably Westerners*, Mitch thought. "Probably from Orange *fucking*

County," he muttered to himself as he looked down at the glass of Liddlesdale and ice before him. He wondered if either of these were fake.

Emily was too young to die, but what is the right age for anyone to leave this planet?

Mitch had seen his fair share of death in his time, and he wasn't happy to see more. Seeing his enemy in combat passing, either in long or close quarters, was less of an ordeal for Mitch; he took it in stride as simply part of the job. Seeing his brothers, sisters, friends, and loved ones leave this world was so much more difficult.

He recalled the kids at school skating on thin ice and never resurfacing from their icy graves. Others met their deaths as a result of motorbikes and teenage inquisitiveness. He recalled the Blues and Royals, making his decision to save his family, then sacrifice his own life on the *Herald of Free Enterprise* to save the lives of others as the ship went down in the English Channel.

He thought about Seray and her beautiful spirit—and Dave. He thought about his cousin's husband and how he had sat in the park, with his suit, no job, and not telling his wife. She didn't know until she and her mum came home and found him strung up in the bathroom.

Graham, the most amazing guy of all time, hung up in his front room, cigarette in his mouth, *fuck you* to the world.

He knew about suicide; he had witnessed it. He had witnessed depression in different states. It was an overdose that eventually killed his father—not a suicide from pity's sake but more a man who knew his place and was comfortable with his decision. He had seen enough, done enough, and it was simply time to move on, at least in his mind. It was time to go.

He also knew brave former soldiers who suffered from depression, an epidemic. In days gone by, including in Mitch's experience, one was expected just to deal with it: get up, dust yourself off, and just get on with it. A dapple of dark humor thrown in was all the rage. Move on.

Mitch also knew that there was a different form of these phenomena, including self-destruction—the feeling a soldier has about being dispensable. Soldiers are, right? Continuing to make battlefield-type sacrifices in civilian life is a form of self-destruction.

He remembered Headley Court, in rehab for a broken knee. The night he arrived, there were no rooms apart from in the Ward, an apparent collective of patients who had witnessed the most death-defying fates. Jilly had fallen off the back of a sofa while babysitting her regimental sergeant major's kids and broken her spine. Jim, a marine, had been hit over the head with a hammer at the Munich Beer Festival and lost his memory. Mike had been shot in the head by a large-caliber bullet, taking away half his head in Iraq. Andy, another marine, had been split in half by a propeller in Chatham, died seven times, and lived to tell the tale.

Andy proudly showed his scars where he had been basically cut in two from his waist to his right shoulder.

The next morning at Headley Court, Mitch looked out the window to see the bizarre sight of their doctor, Arthur Melness, performing Tai Chi on the balcony below him. Mitch felt like he was in a scene of *One Flew over the Cuckoo's Nest*, and maybe he was!

His father had left him with nothing. Mitch had made huge personal and health sacrifices. With the house in Tiburon, his modest British Army pension, and his life insurance, he rested at ease in the knowledge that his wife, Angela, would be fine for the rest of her life and their daughter, Bella, had already made a super start for herself. If she had kids one day, then Mitch's grandchildren would be in good shape too, and maybe further generations to come. He hoped.

He saw an image of himself in an oil painting of Great-Grandad Mitch in the drawing room of an elegant house on a country estate somewhere, with his great-grandchildren and his granddaughter with her Ivy League husband, wearing some pastel Pringle jumper and slippers, looking up at Old Mitch with admiration for starting off the family's wealth trajectory all those years ago.

"Here's to Mitch!" He raised his glass to himself and let out a wry smile. He turned his attention to the band as they came back onstage, ready to half-heartedly serenade the drinkers around him in the Long Bar. He watched as the lead singer continued her smoothing tones to "As Time Goes By." "You must remember this, a kiss is still a kiss, a sigh is just a sigh, as time goes by." He thought the song choice ironic given his memories and his mood tonight. The bass player and pianist strummed away into the night.

He thought about Operation Argus and Jimmy on the RAF extraction flight out of Vilnius, his last words in remembrance of his son.

"Poor fucker," Mitch said aloud.

He thought about how he had witnessed the illusive Conrad Yee dispatch Bokov and Dankov in Moscow three years earlier in December 2016. Yee and Mitch had watched the Mercedes Benz being blown to smithereens, thanks to Yee's improvised antitank mine.

"Fuck you, Dankov," Mitch said to himself before taking another sip of his favorite whisky.

He thought about Jimmy Boyle and his demise at the hands of his own son-in-law, taking over the IRA West Coast operations.

Who knew? "Dirty bastard."

Mitch turned his thoughts to his father, how when he arrived at the hospital, his mother and sister departed the emergency room for Mitch to look down at his dad and see him turn purple, die, revive with each of the huge pulses, his skin turning from pale to purple, dead to alive to dead.

"Brown fucking bread, dead." Mitch had dealt with that a lot in his life so far.

The jazz musicians wrapped up their evening at the Shanghai Club with their translation of another Frank Sinatra tune, "It Was a Very Good Year." Mitch ordered another Dram and headed up to his room, aware of the two men who had been observing him from a dark corner of the bar. "Fucking amateurs," Mitch muttered as he headed through the marble foyer to the elevators. A few moments later, he let himself into the room and turned on the lights.

Mitch's room was a white marble affair with a generous king-size bed and a stunning view of downtown Shanghai with its skyscrapers. The Oriental pearl tower in the middle was lit up in blue and purple like the top of an overelaborate cake at a cheap wedding, standing over eleven hundred feet above the Yangtze River.

His week had been a profitable one, although boring, advising what vehicles, weapons, equipment, and training should be undertaken to become the best and most elite security force in Asia. Not just a mimic, a copy, but the real thing. Mitch wasn't sure if they really had the appetite or if their instincts to just copy would kick in, and all who hired them for their services would be prepared to be disappointed. *Not the best mind-set when real lives are at risk*, he thought.

For a moment, he turned his thoughts to Conrad Yee and how and where he might be. There had been no sightings of him since Moscow.

Then his thoughts went to the love of his life, Bella, and as if by telepathy, his phone buzzed with "Hula Hoopa, thinking of you Dad x," referencing one of the many nicknames he had for his daughter over the years, Ella Bella Super Duper Hula Hoopa.

He called Peggy, his longtime travel agent, to advance his travel arrangements and make the flight changes for the morning, now from Shanghai Pudong Airport to London Heathrow.

Peggy was not just a travel adviser but an arranger of sorts. Mitch and all the team had used her services for years, providing travel arrangements 24/7 and transporting them from one secret place to another, with arrival details, vehicles, hardware, travel documents, even welcome packages with special requests.

She didn't ask questions, just efficiently, securely, and quietely serviced her clientele, all repeat customers, except those she never heard from again.

He then set about sending his text messages to his closest friends and allies for them to gather in London.

Cabo San Lucas, Baja Peninsula, Mexico
2:20 p.m.

Seated in first class at the front of the American Airlines Boeing 737-800, Collins put down his book, *Cold Courage*, as the captain made the announcement that they were about to land in Cabo San Lucas. He stared out the window as the familiar Baja coastline meandered below, edging the desert like lowlands and peaks.

Colonel Collins was meeting with his old friend Lord Jeffry Beecham. Collins was not a colonel, and Beecham not a lord; their nicknames just evolved that way over the years. The pair traversed the world from one highbrow, old-boys party to another, usually involving lots of libation, old stories, and plenty of sandbags. They were both members of the Royal Antigua and Barbuda Rum and Tot Club, and their travels usually involved a sharing of British naval history and a toast to the queen of England promptly at 6:00 p.m. local time, wherever they were in the world.

Beecham was never in the navy, although he was the son of a Royal Naval commander and the brother of a rear admiral. Beecham, however, had friends in high places, and thanks to the company he kept, including sailing around the world for four years on a luxury yacht, he had stints at the British Foreign Office and British Secret Service in hot spots around the world. He was now one of the most eminent authorities on international affairs, criminality, and terrorism, with an international Rolodex with players from both sides of the fence.

Operation Argus had tested Lord Beecham's resolve and resources, and even Collins, after many years of friendship, hadn't realized the extent of the resources available to him.

Collins looked out the window, thinking about Shackleton's somewhat misguided ventures from London to the Antarctic. How his ship, *The Endurance,* was crushed in the sea ice and how he and his men took refuge on Elephant Island. Then how Shackleton and a handful of his men navigated more than eight hundred miles in a converted lifeboat, the *James Caird,* to borrow a ship to return months later to rescue his men. Then, returning to England in the midst of the Great War, Shackleton and his men all went to the war effort to fight for the liberty of Europe.

An amazing story of bravery, determination, and leadership, Collins thought as he saw the coastline before him and Baja California, Mexico. Maybe he would write a book about a similar adventure one day, or maybe one of his own or Beecham's. Between them, they had plenty of tales to tell.

It had been a while since he had been down in Baja, but he had been often enough to have familiarity with the terrain. Beecham had a villa down here, and they often met and hung around Baja, taking trips in Beecham's speed buggy, camping out on the shores of the Sea of Cortez, and having a few beers at Latitude 22, a bar owned by a crusty old mariner, late lunches at the Office, or more libations and fun at Daddy Daycare in town—the code name for the seedy strip joint, a place to leave the husband while the wife shopped at Gucci,

Louis Vuitton, Channel, and Prada in the mall across the road.

As the Boeing landed and taxied toward the steps, Collins checked his phone for messages as his iPhone found the signal, connected, read "Welcome to Telcel," and started downloading.

It had been only a two-and-a-half-hour flight from LAX, so he wasn't expecting too much as the messages came in one by one: the usual junk mail, messages from the office asking him to make simple decisions that they dared not, an invitation to dinner, meet-up for drinks, and then a message that caught his eye—*Business Meeting: Señor Diego Mandito.* He opened the message to find an invitation for this coming Tuesday night. Mandito was the leader of the most powerful cartel in Mexico. Collins held the thought inside to avoid getting indigestion from the mere idea.

The double beep sounded, a signal to take off the seat belt and grab his holdall from above. Doors opened with the warm Cabo air bursting through and the steps down to the tarmac and walk to the terminal. Collins was among the first off the plane and into the terminal. After the long walk to the immigration hall, his passport was stamped and he went out to the plaza where a car was waiting to take him to Beecham's residence.

Collins opened the rear passenger-side door, tossed his carry-on on the seat beside him, and said, "Right then. Let's get going. Don't want to be late for my meeting."

As the driver pulled away from the airport, Collins thought about the last time he had seen Beecham, in London at the Union Club, a farewell dinner after what was a very sad affair. Old friends gathered to remember some of the friends lost along the way. One by one, they had gone their own ways, with—as usually was the case—Beecham and Collins being the last ones to leave and pick up the tab.

Beecham was an old friend, a good friend, and a drinking partner. Banter, politics, economics, the state of the world now, the history of wars in the past hundred years, planes, trains, and automobiles, distant lands, discovered places, undiscovered worlds, exploits, achievements, mountains climbed, rivers crossed, stories of new and stories of old.

There certainly was never a dull moment to be had in the company of Lord Jeffry Beecham and Colonel Collins.

Collins stared out the window of the town car as they passed through Cabo and the million-dollar yachts in the marina to his left and the dollar shops to his right. Two cruise ships anchored in the harbor were towering above the luxury duty-free shopping on portside, Daddy Daycare on his right, where he and Beecham had gone on his last trip.

He knew that most of the town on the peninsula was owned by the cartels and a way for them to invest their billions into legitimate businesses and come out clean with tourist dollars in their bank accounts. There was an unwritten law between them to keep Cabo clean and avoid turf wars on the shore; none of them wanted to frighten the tourists away, as they needed to legitimize their business operations.

"Diego Mandito? What the hell would Diego Mandito want with us?" he asked himself aloud.

Judging by his previous history with Mandito, Collins knew that nothing good would come from this encounter.

Whenever the señor was involved, there was a trail of dead bodies too.

William & Victoria's Restaurant
Harrogate, North Yorkshire, United Kingdom
12:30 p.m.

Life was good for Bob, having taken over Grace & Co following the mysterious demise of its two founders, Harrison and Grace. One was impaled on a piece of rebar, evidently having fallen to his death from the top of his own construction site, and the other died in his 6-Series BMW, with his stupid fucking mullet haircut and enough heroin to kill an elephant.

Bob had taken over the firm and invested some of his accumulation from the British Gas & Pipeline Corporation in a nice property. He had a very amenable female companion and, thanks to Sara, a ready-made social network of cool, down-to-earth, worldly, and wise people—just how he liked it.

During his military career, with the Special Air Service, he had built a reputation that even in that context attracted his nickname, Big Bad Bob. After service, he had gone on to various security gigs, his last one with the British Gas & Pipeline Corporation in Equatorial Guinea.

He was never one for being frivolous with his money and had already built a tidy sum. No girlfriends of any substance to speak of, at least until now, no family, just Bob in this big, wide world. His gig with the BGPC had paid him handsomely, and his need for serious work had diminished, but he still liked to keep his hand in the game.

The lunch rush was on at William & Victoria's Restaurant, a place Big Bad Bob had come to love for the fish 'n' chips whenever he was in the UK. He had some in front of him, along with a refreshing brew. As he ate, he glanced casually around the room, taking in the regulars, who were known as the crew, and keeping an eye out for anyone who looked suspicious. The crew was an eclectic mix—a couple of property developers, an actress, a racehorse owner, a barrister, a steel broker, a construction entrepreneur, and of course Sara, his newly acquired girlfriend, partner, and social acquaintance, but Bob was thinking she was growing into much more, which was a new experience for him.

The conversation in the restaurant dipped in and out of world politics, local gossip, new projects, lessons from old, travels gone by, and travel to come. It was a very convivial crowd, and Bob could skate on the surface without getting into too much detail about his past. Bob guessed that suited everyone around the table as they enjoyed one another's company and the delightful Yorkshire fayre.

Grace & Co had settled down again after their unexpected loss of the founders, trying to work out exactly what it was that they did and who they did it for. A business consultancy, buying and selling businesses, supported by corporate finance, marketing, sales, and administration, it was a small but effective team, and with the stench of Harrison and Grace now gone, it was a much better place to be.

With Dankov's demise in Moscow, the casino acquisition business had dried up, so the need to be in Leeds opposite

Dankov's casino was no longer required. So Bob acquired an office suite on the grounds of Ripley Castle to set up shop and call it home—an easy ten-minute drive in his new Aston Martin DB-9 from his swanky apartment on the Stray.

He looked over at Sara as he reflected on his own journey, his time in the army, Special Air Service, his rise through the ranks in civilian life, and recognition as the Fixer. He thought about Equatorial Guinea and the shithole of a job and country. He thought about Hamza Malik and BGPC. He thought about Jimmy, Mitch, Sam, Ryan, and Mac. He thought about his life, his journey, still looking at Sara as she talked and jived and joked, and he felt the most at home he had ever felt. He had never felt this way before.

Sara had had her trials and tribulations too. Never married, not quite. She had a series of men in her life who had promised a lot and given her little but heartache and bad memories. In the short time he had been with her, they had grown together. He needed her warmth, kindness, and loving, and she had needed his strength and character.

They were right for each other; he knew that, and that is why he had been to see Sir Thomas earlier in the week about booking his castle for their wedding. She didn't know; he hadn't told her yet. He would do so in due course, when the time was right, when he was ready. It wouldn't be long, he thought.

The crew was listening to Alan as he finished his story about a local celebrity at a local charity dinner who had shouted out in the middle of an auction to the auctioneer, "I'll give you a fucking hundred thousand pounds if you stop fucking my wife!" The auction audience was mesmerized, as if this was some sick joke, but the majority of the audience, including the husband, the wife, and the auctioneer, knew it was true!

Although they all knew the story, Alan's comedic execution drew them all into a raucous round of laughter once more at the expense of the auctioneer, his wife, the husband, and probably his wife too.

"I bet that was a fun taxi ride home for them all," observed Paul with his even drier humor.

At that, Bob's phone buzzed with a message. "I need you to get to London, day after tomorrow?"

Bob knew who the message was from. He replied, "Yes. Time. Place. Dress?"

"The Union. As soon as you can get there, Bond," came the reply.

He knew that the fun tonight would end. And he also knew that tonight, probably at the Ivy, just him and Sara, he would pop the question over a nightcap.

Bob wasn't a fearful type of guy. His history spoke for itself, but this was something he had never done before, new territory for Big Bad Bob.

He turned his thoughts back to the text message.

"What the fuck is that all about?" he muttered to himself.

"And Bond?" As in *James Bond*. He laughed. "Fucking buffoon."

6
DAD

Washington, DC, United States
8:00 a.m.

BELLA MADE HER WAY THROUGH the final mile to the office, passing the street vendors getting ready for the influx of tourists to sell their wares to. She got to Washington Circle, headed down Twenty-Third, and turned left by the Washington Monument and run-down Constitution Avenue, with the museums on her right and the White House to her left. It was fairly warm for the time of year, but Bella could still feel the bite of the cold wind sweeping down Chesapeake Bay from the north. The winter sun was out, shining down on the White House, lighting her up like a jewel. She had rested the day before, at home, chilling out, getting a good night's sleep, but the parting reference from the youth on the night of the incident was on her mind. "Who the fuck were *they*?"

There was something about Washington, DC, that felt comfortable to Bella. She always felt a sense of order there, a feeling of calm and a sense of purpose being in Washington with all its diplomats, civil servants, and lawyers. In her current role, Bella sort of transcended all three—working out where the next big geopolitical risks might be, as well as opportunities, and in some instances, boots on the ground and getting her hands dirty.

Brexit was an issue representing instability not only in Europe but potential global economic uncertainty too. No doubt, as the Russians had meddled with the 2016 presidential election, there was Putin's fingerprints on this too.

The use of social media to meddle with geopolitical stability was on the rise and now the new weapon in the arsenal of war—a secret, clandestine war with a generous serving of maskirovka on top. It was the principle of layering lie upon lie upon lie so that no one knows what the truth is anymore, and quickly the audience's attention span dries up, and it becomes like watching a soap opera, when in fact it's real people's lives that are at stake.

Increasing violence in Mexico and Central and South America, fueled by the cartels, with twenty-nine thousand killings alone last year, one every fifteen minutes.

The continued occupation of Crimea. The instability in Venezuela.

All, in Bella's view, ultimately driven by greed and the desire for power and the combination of the two.

In other words, business was booming.

From her father's perspectives on global politics and events and insights, Bella had grown a passion for understanding and working out the intricacies of global affairs. She studied at Oxford, Lady Magdalen's College, and then went on to join the start-up, Executive Outcomes, a platform that gathered international, regional, and local news and events, and through artificial intelligence had an algorithm to make geopolitical predictions and risk analyses for corporations and investors.

The whole Argus debacle had taught her more than she realized at the time.

Nikita, her old school friend from Oxford, and at many points potential romantic interest somehow, thanks to his mother, Viktoria, got wrapped up in the now infamous First World Bank investment scheme, cleverly created by Dmitri Dankov of the Russian dark underground and funded and to the benefit of the Russian state. It was initially created to get cash back into the cash-starved nation, but over time, it became a very lucrative funding mechanism built on money laundering through casinos around the world, partnering with and facilitating drug distribution networks, and then evolving into taking big bets on geopolitical outcomes that, unknown to anyone outside the inner circle, had been manipulated from seemingly unpredictable outcomes to sure bets for First World Bank.

Her beloved Nikita got caught right in the middle—the result of a mother's ambition for her son. Nikita was the puppet, originally taking credit for his mercurial predictions until he realized the depth of the conspiracy and deceit.

He was just the messenger boy, and when he found out, when he discovered his mother in her swanky London residence, eyes gouged out, in a pool of blood, in her own version of the Amber Room, it all dawned on him before returning to flat 1b, and the rest is history.

Apart from the sadness, she had learned how corruption is everywhere, around every corner, under every stone, with greed and power at the heart of the motivation. It was the innocent who always suffered, and that was why Bella was in this business—for the naïve, the innocent, the vulnerable.

Despite the February chill, Bella felt sweat trickle down her back as she jogged to her office. She knew she was good-looking enough to turn heads, that her long mane of golden-brown hair got the attention of men and women alike. At five feet ten with the build of a cross-country runner, she was a presence whenever she entered a room, and she knew it.

She pulled up to the revolving doors of her office building, flashed her card at the familiar security guard, and strolled right into the elevator bank and the fourth floor.

Deidre was at the reception, always early, bright, and cheerful, no matter what was going on.

"He's in his office, waiting to see you, Bella." She smiled and waved her down the hallway.

"Thanks, Deidre. Love the nail polish." She smiled as she breezed past.

Deputy assistant director at the Central Intelligence Agency was a big thing. Twenty years of dedicated service, loyalty in the ranks, and keeping your nose clean would take care of that. Bella knocked politely, waited for the nod, and then walked right in.

Deputy Assistant Director, DAD, Chip Brown III had been around the block a few times, and his face showed it. "A scar for every year of service," he would say as a standing joke. Usually a very casual, lighthearted guy, he saw the humor in even the most macabre of situations (which they came across a lot), but he clearly wasn't in his bright and breezy mood today.

He turned to look at her.

"What the hell happened on Saturday night, *d'Artagnan?*"

"What do you mean?" She realized it was pointless to bluff at this point. "Oh, you mean the incident?"

"The *incident?*" he shouted. "Yes, Bella, the *incident*. The fifth fucking *incident* this year, Bella."

She stared right back. "Self-defense, boss."

"Self-fucking-defense, Bella? We have another two hospitalized thugs, one in a fucking coma, the other with a broken skull, with the third youth scared shitless! And you call that self-fucking-defense?

"What is it with you? Five times this year. Little Miss Bella finds herself in difficulty and devastates her way out of it, usually resulting in the alleged perpetrators in the hospital. Seriously in the hospital.

"Isn't it about time you took up bear fighting or something equally violent as a hobby, as opposed to picking on these poor fucking criminals?" Chip shouted with a grin.

Bella maintained her stare into his eyes.

"Seriously, you need to stop that. One day, it could misfire. You know that. Why do you do it? Is that what women do nowadays for fun?"

Bella knew the seriousness of his message, and she knew that she might have to curtail her newly discovered sport.

"Bella, you really should consider going to see one of the counselors."

Bella just looked at him deadpan. No answer.

They looked at each other for a moment. Bella knew they shared a common bond between them, her father, Mitch. Mutual respect had been earned over years. That common bond would stand between her and trouble … this time. Again, she suddenly felt the strange feeling that something was not right.

"You find out anything about the guys involved?" she asked. "The third one said something that sounded an awful lot like I've got a hit out on me."

Chip frowned. "Yeah, we don't like the sounds of this. Got nothing yet. The FBI is assisting us on the domestic front." He hesitated. "I'll let you know more as soon as we find out anything. But, hey, Bella, it's lucky that you haven't actually killed any of them. Too much fucking paperwork for me." He half grinned, recovering from the seriousness of the moment, reaching over to Bella, opening his arms, and giving Bella a fatherly hug. Bella hugged Chip back. They were more than colleagues; they were family. Chip was Bella's second dad.

"What the hell are you thinking, Bella? You know there's only so many times I can sweep stuff like this under the carpet."

"I know, I know," Bella responded. "You're the best." She winked at him with her big hazel eyes.

Clearing his throat, Chip said, "Okay, moving on, Bella, we have had more intel coming from our friends in Somalia and a continued buildup of hardware. In addition to the three HC-130s, various armored vehicles, weaponry, ammunition—enough to support a small army."

"All from the inventory lost or misplaced in Iraq?" Bella asked with a knowing smile.

"Yep, that would be the one," Chip retorted.

"Do we know who the collectors are?"

"No. But we traced the funding."

"Where from?" Bella showed her impatience with Chip's tease. "Come on, Chip!"

She could tell that Chip was enjoying his moment of the reveal.

"As always, the trail was complicated. At first look, it seems like the usual suspects, the Russians, but what would they need in investing in old-inventory US military hardware? Russia was just a channel it would seem. At least one major source of the funds is coming from Mexico."

Bella gave Chip a deadpan stare as though he had lost his mind. "Mexico? What would the Mexicans want with used US military hardware in Africa?" she said, not believing the intel but catching herself in front of her boss, her friend, and leader of her CIA fan club.

"It's not just Mexico itself. It's better than that. It's the Mexican cartels," Chip stated with a cold smile.

"What the hell does that mean?' asked Bella.

"For you to find out, young lady. Now, no more *incidents*, okay?"

"Right," she said, and headed for the door.

7
MONKEY PUZZLE

George Bush Center for Intelligence
Special Operations Unit, Langley,
Virginia, United States
8:00 a.m.

BELLA WAS ABSORBED IN THIS latest monkey puzzle—a mounting arsenal of military equipment, including wings capable of taking approximately four hundred soldiers anywhere within a four-thousand-mile radius of the stash without refueling. The target could be anywhere across north and middle Africa, the Middle East, or even southern Europe. What could be the possible target? And why the Mexican cartels?

Getting supply routes for narcotics to Europe through Africa was common ground, but this was the wrong side of Africa. Why would the drug traffickers want equipment for a small army? What were the Mexicans up to with the wrong type of equipment, the wrong side of the world, and the wrong side of Africa? It just didn't add up. Bella scratched her head while sipping her Peet's coffee.

She knew that Africa was a hotbed of interest for numerous interested parties keen to unlock the long-term potential of the continent, with China and Russia taking the lead in that interest—the race to colonize Africa. She knew from her research that Russia already had long-term interests in the likes of Angola, Mozambique, Guinea-Bissau, Democratic Republic of Congo, Egypt, Somalia, Ethiopia, Uganda, and Benin.

But why the Mexicans? It didn't make sense yet. But she would work out this puzzle.

She knew from her Argus experience that narcs needed new ways to launder and legitimize money—turning dirty money into good. Clean money was a priority, and despite their home-grown casinos, convenience stores, restaurants, and resorts in Mexico, ever more creative ways to distance themselves from their core business was always a good thing, at least in her mind.

She also knew that foreign sovereign states, including Russia, held a strong desire for foreign currency.

Just like Argus, she saw the lengths that people, organizations, and sovereign states would go in that quest.

She thought again about Nikita, as she often did, and how she had found him at his apartment on Bromley High Street, strung up, warm but dead. She discouraged the single tear from her eye as she recalled her attempts to try to force and pump the life back into him. It was still a painful memory. It always would be. The flashbacks had become less intense, as had the nightmares, but they were still present in her life. She imagined that these would go away at some point, unlike the pain over Nikita's murder. In her moment of self-reflection, she wondered if she was suffering from posttraumatic stress disorder. She wondered if Chip was right and she should seek counseling instead of telling herself that she could handle it.

Focus, girl! she thought.

As she figured through this conundrum, she thought about the elements: military arsenal, Mexican cartels, range, purpose. It still didn't make any sense.

Chip breezed into the operations room, two Starbucks in his hand. At Bella's stand-up desk, he handed her the double-shot vente latte and took a sip of his own.

"What's up, Chip? Why the serious face?"

"How's the puzzle coming along?" he responded.

"It's weird. Any news on the three musketeers?"

Chip looked at her again.

"What is it, Chip?" She took a sip of coffee and stared back at him, sensing he had something serious to say.

It had been a long morning already, and this puzzle in front of her was grating her. Bella was used to working things out, connecting the dots, solving the puzzle. Why the Mexicans? It just didn't make sense. Or did it?

Chip slid a brown envelope across the desk. Bella looked down at the envelope and back up to Chip. "What's this?" she asked as she opened it to reveal a dozen black-and-white photos.

The first was a picture of Goldtooth and his injuries, the next was of number two with his battered face and cauliflower ear, and the third was of the youth. She looked at Chip with an inquiring look and then back at the stack of photos: what looked like a CCTV image of a man talking to Goldtooth, then a photograph of a backpack with a wedge of greenbacks next to it, then a picture of Bella walking out her front door in her jogging gear.

"What the fuck is this, Chip?"

Chip looked at his coffee. "Well, Bella, let me tell you. I think—no, *we* think—that there might be more to this than meets the eye. The FBI managed to track down the third guy. Thank God the security cameras in the bar were working. We got good images of him. Turns out he has a record. He was pretty easy to locate after the FBI went looking."

Bella leaned forward in her seat and clasped both hands together in front of her.

"When the FBI searched his apartment, they found that backpack with $20,000 in it. At first, we just assumed it was drug money, but then we found the picture of you by your front door and a betting slip from the Vanguard Casino in National Harbor."

The hairs on the back of Bella's neck stood on end as though a ghost had just walked in the room.

"You mean Dankov's newest casino in DC? I thought he was fucking dead!"

Chip nodded. "We thought so too."

"The CCTV image is from their security system. The two men in the picture are Samuel Johnson, otherwise known as multiple felon and drug dealer, Goldtooth."

"And the other?" Bella asked, losing her patience.

"That is Ivan Manovich, number one in Dankov's operations in the US."

Bella stared back at him, another puzzle to rack her brain, but this one was much closer to home. Her mind raced, and she recollected when, as a child, Dankov's people took her from school to that apartment, holding her ransom. Her father and Dankov had crossed paths too many times, and their rivalry had spilled over beyond professional rivalry.

"What does this mean?" asked Bella. "This isn't the usual Russian way. If they wanted me dead, they wouldn't send three druggies to do the job."

"Seems from the youth, they didn't want you dead. He was the camera man."

For the second time in as many minutes, her skin went as cold as ice. She didn't need to ask what the camera was for. She understood. She got it. Their motive was to leave permanent scars and ultimately to inflict pain on Mitch.

"But I thought Dankov was dead." She shook her head in disbelief.

"He should be. We're looking into that right now."

"For fuck's sake, Chip" was all Bella could say.

"Stay safe, Bella. We will have someone tailing you from now on. At least for the next few days. Bob Smart from operations. I think you know him?"

Bella nodded as Chip breezed back out of the office.

"Thanks for that, Chip! Happy fucking birthday to you too!" Bella mumbled to herself.

At 4:00 p.m., she ran the ten miles to her apartment to get showered, changed, and ready for her date later that evening. She would be heading a little out of her way to Mount Pleasant and the newly acclaimed restaurant, Elle. She kind of liked the name, so that was good enough for her.

She had spotted Bob Smart following her on a bicycle, sticking out like a sore thumb. *Not so fucking smart,* she thought, but she appreciated the extra pair of eyes nevertheless.

At thirty-three, Wills was a little older than Bella, but they had grown up with a lot in common. Both their fathers were from the British military, and neither Wills nor Bella really knew them, as they were often absent. They both had been educated in England, Bella at Oxford and Wills at Imperial College London, Material Science, and then on to a commissioned role with the British Army, Intelligence Corps, specializing in geopolitical issues, and had been posted to DC for the past eighteen months.

Their paths had crossed, they got along, and their intellects were equally sharp, as was their desire to find themselves, their fathers, and their place in the world.

Although a tad intense, Wills reminded her of someone, perhaps Nikita. She had loved Nikita, and maybe Wills was a replacement—a dubious honor for Wills, who Bella suspected maybe just wanted Bella for himself.

She got to her apartment front door, the bleached blood in her pathway still visible and the monkey wrench still in its place. Bob was now across the street in a black Buick. Bella smiled as she thought of the stereotypical comedies about undercover agencies. Bob could have been in one of those shows. Perhaps tomorrow he would be wearing a beige raincoat and a trilby and donning a moustache. She chuckled.

Her phone buzzed. It was Mitch. "I need you in London tomorrow night. Text me when you get in."

"Crikey!" she muttered. "Change of plans." She hurried inside and took care of business, which included showering, packing, and letting Wills know she wouldn't make it. She also texted Chip to let him know she had to go to London. He texted back that he wanted to send an agent with her for her own protection.

"No, that's okay, Chip," she said. "I'll be just fine on my own."

Chengkoucun
People's Republic of China
5:45 p.m.

Chengkoucun was a small coastal town overlooking the Matsu islands across the South China Sea and spanning the neck of the headland leading to the ancient city of Dinghai. The town on either side touched the ocean, with the fishing community having access from both sides. At the southwest corner of the town, half a dozen properties overlooked the beach and the fishing boats below.

The middle house—a dark wood timber affair with a wraparound porch, bamboo gardens, and neatly kept lawns—stood out for its neatness and attention to detail in this traditional Chinese town, where busy people went around the latest hustle and bustle in their strive for survival.

This home was clearly owned by someone with exquisite attention to detail, an obsessive-compulsive disorder, too much time on their hands, or a combination of all three.

As the sun set, the house was quiet, with only the faint noise of the bamboo fluttering in the wind like a serenade.

The windows were open, with the breeze flapping the wisp-like curtains and the pungent smell of smoke in the air. Inside, the candles flickered as the light faded outside. A kettle on the stove whistled as the steam evaporated, almost empty.

This was the home of the most notorious and prolific assassin of the century. Under a shroud of utmost secrecy, he had completed many missions on behalf of his adopted country, China, before going freelance to the highest bidder. Finding peace and tranquility in Brisbane, Australia, he was compromised during Operation Argus and moved to China to downplay his career. He could retire and be somewhat safe from his enemies. Or so he thought.

In the main room, on a chair, a man sat silently, cold, staring at the ceiling with a simple but telling red dot in the middle of the forehead, the cushions behind him absorbing the explosion of blood, skull, and brains from the exit wound from the high-caliber single bullet. His eyes were wide open, above the high cheekbones, and he was dressed in his traditional Chinese robes.

Two framed pictures stood behind him on the cabinet, one of his wife, Mingh, and their son, Bingwen. The other was of four young boys growing up in the Lake District, one of them Conrad Yee, from times long past.

He sat there motionless as the kettle steamed the last drop and the whistling stopped.

Conrad Yee, 狗, Gǒu, the Dog's chapter was over. Old scores had been settled.

8

RED DAHLIAS

October 2017
Petrovskie Vorota Medical Center
Koloboskiv, Moscow
2:00 p.m.

THE RUSSIAN OFFICIAL CONSIDERED THE situation as he took the seven-minute ride in his black Mercedes S-Class to the hospital. The driver and close-protection guard were in the front, and three other cars were in close proximity, full of muscle in crumpled black suits, white shirts, black ties, and earpieces.

The cavalcade sped through the Moscow streets at a pace not fast enough to be reckless, not too slow that it was exposed. Just purposeful.

As they arrived at the main entrance, the men in suits got out first, surveying the area before opening the rear door of the S-Class and steering the passenger into the building. The heightened intensity of security raised interest, given that, after all, this was Moscow, with more than one hundred and fifty thousand cameras, only a mile and a half from the Kremlin, the FSB on every street corner. This was as much a show as anything, as the passenger was in safe territory—his territory, his homeland.

In his long black Siberian wool coat, the single figure walked ahead down the long, wide, marble-floored corridor. At just five foot seven, he was dwarfed by his bodyguards but walked with a swagger of a self-confident, successful, powerful man. The man in black entered the room with two of the close-protection operatives falling in line outside.

The hospital bed was surrounded by gadgets with various charts, graphs, digital outputs, and a rhythm of beats and pings. The man in the bed, dressed in green robes, was tall, dark, and imposing, despite his prone position. The doctor in his white coat stood attentively by the side of the bed, complete with a clipboard in hand.

"Dobroye utro, ser." He clicked his heels as he spoke.

"Utro," responded the man in the woolen coat.

The room was typically sparse, like any hospital room in Moscow, but there was a distinct lack of flowers, cards, and well-wishers. In the three months since he had been in the room, he had received no visitors. The Russian official knew the person he was visiting would not want any as soon as he realized his current condition was irreversible. He'd come out of the coma only yesterday, after three months in the hospital. Frankly, he couldn't blame the man if he chose to off himself instead of living the way he would have to live for the rest of his miserable life.

"How is he?"

"As I'm sure you've been informed, he came out of the coma last night, sir. It's a miracle that he is still alive. Lucky that his door wasn't fully secured, as we believe that his seat belt was trapped in the door. As a result, he was blown clear of the car, out the door at the point of explosion."

"Is he able to talk yet?"

"He is weak. He uttered a couple of words last night. We have confirmed that he has limited or no cognitive damage and expect that he will be fully recovered in the next couple of months, at least mentally. He lost his right leg at the groin, broke his right arm, which has now healed, and the scars to his face and burns to his upper right torso, although healed, will remain."

"What did he have to say?" asked the man in the woolen coat.

"Ty, blyad! Sir." *You fucker.*

The man in the woolen coat let out a side smile and twinkled his eyes in true admiration of the Russian, blown to smithereens, still defiant, still Russian in the face of adversity. That was the Russian way. That made him proud of this patriot before him.

"Thank you, Doctor. Keep up the good work. Make sure we give this man the best care in Moscow, in Russia, the best care we have in the empire. Keep me appraised. I want to know his speed of recovery. I want him back on his feet as soon as possible." He let out a cold smile, understanding the gravity of his humor.

"Yes, sir!"

The man in the woolen coat passed over the bunch of Russian red dahlias, a deep symbol of Russian loyalty and respect. He smiled at the doctor, shook hands, and left the same way in which he came.

February 2019
Institute of Directors
116 Pall Mall, London
11:45 a.m.

James Digby strolled into the reception at 116 Pall Mall with its double-balustrade staircase emerging from the polished, white-and-black seamed marble below. It was adorned with oil paintings of London and notorieties past, a pair of Chippendale chairs, a Louis XV sideboard with a singular, matching clock.

The Directors Room was a century-old London traditional meeting place, like that of a giant chess room with a sea of tables, for two, a place to do deals.

Digby, in his red cavalry twill trousers, perfectly hemmed to his Church's brogues, his pink, double-cuffed, Chelsea collar shirt, and his Barbour jacket, looked just the part, topped off with his Selfridges umbrella, his Bremont watch, and his happy but confident demeanor.

He entered the Directors Room and quickly found his appointment, one Vladimir Vostok, Federal Security Service, FSB, of the Russian Federation, representative in the United Kingdom, unofficial mouthpiece of Putin himself, and Digby's contact in London.

They often chose to meet here for its very public nature, its history, and the play on a chess room, as they regularly exchanged their coded banter and played their own version of chess, just on a much more important scale, as some would say.

Digby, a former subaltern of the Blues and Royals, Household Cavalry enjoyed his stint at Knightsbridge, his private family allowance, and his current job deep inside the corridors of the Foreign Office. Vostok, a former KGB commander, grew up in the ranks as Putin shot to fame and power and remained a loyal friend and trusted operative for sensitive tasks and situations. More recently, he was located almost entirely in London, with the occasional trip back to the motherland and Moscow.

"Hello, Vlad, old boy, How the devil are you? It's been a while!" Digby stepped up to the small square table and reached out his hand.

Vostok looked up from his newspaper with disdain and motioned for Digby to sit.

"*Syad*, Digby."

"So, what do I owe this pleasure, my fair-feathered friend?" Although Vostok had initiated the meeting, Digby had his own agenda too. What the fuck were the Russians doing building up forces in the DRC?

Vostok in his dark gray, cheap suit, white shirt, black tie, and garishly bright gold Rolex on his wrist, looked like an archetypal depiction of a Russian spy from an 80s' film or *Tintin* comic book. Digby despised most Russians, especially Vostok and his crowd, but despite that, he also had a strange tinge of respect for them in their endeavors of defeating Hitler, losing millions of people, soldiers and civilians, in one of the most hard-fought battles of any war, the siege of Leningrad, 872 days and probably the longest and most destructive sieges in history, of any war, anywhere. Digby figured that they deserved some respect for that. It was their pure, unfiltered arrogance that he detested.

The man in the cheap suit pushed a yellow envelope Digby's way. Digby looked at it. "What's this, my friend?"

"Open it, and you will see."

Inside, there were two grainy black-and-white photos of two men, who looked to be in their late forties, and a younger woman.

"Nice picture, Vlad, especially the one on the right," he said, pointing to the woman in the picture, who was tall, lean, and incredibly beautiful. "As I said, what is this?"

"These three were at the last place two of our operatives were seen alive. They have now disappeared from the face of the earth—no contact, no nothing, presumed either captured or dead," Vostok said without a smile and not short of a tone of menace.

"How would I know who they are? Even if we could decipher these cheap CCTV screen shots," Digby countered.

"The two operatives have friends in high places, and we thought you might be able to help track their whereabouts."

"Well, Vlad, as always, we will see what we can do. Always happy to oblige, old boy." Digby put the photographs back into the envelope and pushed it back over the chess table to Vostok.

Vostok nodded slowly, looking at Digby in the eyes with his combination of distrust and dislike.

"Now, all is fair, one favor for another. I have a question of my own."

"What is it?" Vostok asked in his monotone voice.

"My friends in high places are wondering what you chaps are doing building up forces in the DRC. The Congo seems a bit out of your way, doesn't it?"

It was well known that both Russia and China had designs on Africa as a largely untapped continent, with opportunities to build alliances and assets on the continent for their long-term game plan. Much of the continent remained disorganized chaos, but the future potential was significant.

Vostok looked carefully at Digby for a few uncomfortable seconds, smiled, and responded, "We are interested in the long-term peace and stability of Africa much more so than you English ever have been over the past two hundred years—cleaning up after you killed, conquered, raped, and left. We have friends in Africa, and we offer our support."

"What the fuck does that really mean, Vostok?"

The relationship between the two had dwindled over recent months, as had the one between their two countries. Accusations of Vostok's team conducting various overt, covert, and not so covert assassinations had been highly publicized.

Sergai Skripa, father, and his daughter, Yulia, were just one high-profile example that made the national and international press. They were poisoned in Salisbury with the nerve agent Novichok, or A-234.

These daylight misdemeanors, including infringements of airspace, displays of Russian naval firepower in British waters, and shallowly disguised business dealings to take over British infrastructure, were just ways in which to say *fuck you* to the Western world, or as they say in Russian, *Yebat Tebya.*

The other thing about these Russians was, as Digby had learned, you just never quite knew the difference between truth and lies, a state that he had come to know as maskirovka.

Given the way the conversation was going, they came to a halt. Digby had no inclination to get indigestion over lunch. He thanked Vostok and went off to enjoy lunch on his own at the Restaurant. He had seen some of his favorites on the menu, and a nice glass of Pouilly-Fume would erase the unpleasantries that were Vostok, at least until next time.

Following these types of learn-a-little, usually short and terse meetings, Digby often wondered what the point was. It was like a little game of cat and mouse—never give too much away. The questions that were asked were not questions but more warnings that "We already know the answer." It was a strange world.

Digby knew exactly who the three in the photographs were. He also knew who the victims were, and he knew about the very efficient cleanup operation conducted at the Fox & Hounds. "Fucking Ruskies," Digby said to himself as he savored his first sip of his favorite wine, slightly raising his glass to Waterloo Place out the window, trying to put the unsavoriness of Vostok out of his mind. He also knew the girl in the photograph, Bella Mitchell, half-British, US citizen, daughter of a former SAS operator, and now fully fledged member of the Central Intelligence Agency. She was indeed a *stunner*, as his old school chums would have said.

Digby had met Bella briefly in Washington, six months previously. Over his lunch, he racked his brains to see how he could engineer another encounter, although her reputation came before her about her like for dispatching victims, including the latest two across the city in Chelsea.

Digby accidently knocked his glass of wine on the linen tablecloth, tipping it over, but with his quick reaction, he caught the glass before it was a total spill. He grabbed his napkin and mopped up the quarter-of-a-glass spillage, shaking his head, thinking of Bella, her beauty and her distraction. "Bloody fool," he muttered to himself as the waiter delivered his usual, sole meunière.

9
RISE AND FALL

June 1975
Leningrad State University
United Soviet Social Republic
11:30 a.m.

KOSTAS DANKOV STOOD WITH THE rest of the class of 1975 on the grounds of Leningrad State University, ready to have the ceremonial photo taken that would mark the end of five years of hard study to graduate from law school. He glanced over at his friend, Vladimir Putin, and shot him a smile. Vlad grinned back. Dankov could barely contain his excitement. He liked learning, although much of Russian law was boring and didn't matter much anyway, but he was anxious to begin what he hoped would be a prosperous career.

As Dankov stood with his classmates, he felt confident that his family connections would make a rise to the top fairly easy. The Dankov-Putin connection would become quite important; of that he was sure.

Putin was the youngest of three children, but his two older brothers died, one as an infant and the other of diphtheria during the siege of Leningrad. His mother was a factory worker, and his father a conscript submariner for the Soviet Navy until his transfer to the regular army, where he was severely wounded in 1942. Putin's grandmother and maternal uncles were also killed during that time by the Germans. Putin went on to study German, speaking fluently, and learned judo, becoming a black belt before arriving at the university and meeting his friend, Kostas Dankov.

Dankov's family had also seen hard times, with him losing his mother in a bombing raid and his father in the frozen trenches during the siege. He was raised by his grandmother, and by the time he was eighteen, he was already a father to Stella and then shortly later, Dmitri Dankov.

University had been hard, trying to provide for the family and study at the same time. Some of Dankov's extracurricular activities fell outside of the principles he was learning at law school, but then again, this was the Soviet Union, and rules, although rigid, were often liberally applied.

It was these struggles, making ends meet and survival, that defined his ethos in doing what he had to do to survive—an ethos that would be adopted by his children in their future careers.

The years passed, and Dankov did rise to the top. However, to his surprise, it wasn't within the law. He joined Putin in attending the 401st KGB school in Okhta close by, and he and his friend launched their careers with the Komitet Gosudarstvennoy Iezopasnosti, the KGB.

After their initial training, Dankov lost track of Putin. Their paths did not cross again until nine years later in Dresden, East Germany. Vladimir was a translator, Kostas was an intelligence officer, and the Berlin Wall was about to collapse along with the Soviet Empire.

February 2019
Casa Panorama
Cabo San Lucas, Baja Peninsula, Mexico
4:00 p.m.

Señor Diego Mandito sat in his villa, Casa Panorama, which sat on the cliff on the south side of Cabo San Lucas, overlooking the Paraiso Escondido and the Pacific Ocean. Nothing stood between the villa and Japan but the ocean and whales. It was a scene of seemingly never-ending tranquility. Nothing was in proximity; just the villa sat on its perch— quiet, peaceful, and private.

Dressed in his immaculate linen suit and a purple paisley cravat, Mandito looked out at his piece of the world, reminding himself of where he had come from and where he had been as he was passed his glass of Patron en Lalique, the best tequila, matured in Bourbon, French Oak, served up in the Baccarat Harmonie tumbler with a single large cube of ice and a single string of lime skin.

The son of a car mechanic, Diego Mandito grew up in Mexico City, skipping school and helping his father in his shop. A handful of cars a week was a steady stream of work, and income didn't seem to grow too much, but as their apparent wealth bloomed, he got involved in the family business at a tender fourteen years old. He quickly picked up that there was much more valuable merchandise in the cars than the cars themselves.

His father had learned the skills required trying to scratch out a legitimate living at one of the US car-manufacturing plants. He started their fledgling business as a repair shop, developing it into a makeover shop to bring aging cars back to life, then applying those skills to pack an otherwise normal-looking vehicle with an additional one thousand pounds of white, powdery merchandise.

That was in the early days when sophistication of detection was limited, but of course, they had to evolve to keep ahead of the game.

His father was shot and killed when Diego was just eighteen, and as the oldest brother of four, he took over the family business and quickly expanded operations beyond being the mule to becoming one of the largest, most feared and ruthless cartels in Mexico City.

Diego was savvy and understood that the power of compromise and alliances was far more productive than the power of guns and war, forging partnerships with other cartels and government agencies and making friends in high places. Many say in Mexico that Mandito coined the phrase, "I am a lover, not a fighter." This was his mantra, but ultimately, he knew that to be successful and to survive, he had to be ruthless too—which he was.

He sat under the cabana of Casa Panorama, next to the pool, sipping his tequila, smoking his Gurkha Black Dragon cigar, looking out across the Pacific and thinking.

Over the years, he had diversified, as he knew this to be the future of business and a way to mask the roots of his own core business. His conglomerate now owned the largest portfolio of convenience stores in Mexico—a great way to turn dirty money into clean and primarily a cash business too. Perfect.

He had invested in construction companies, that in turn built his property developments and investments and owned twenty luxury hotel properties across Mexico and Central America. He had purchased a small chain of gas stations, added convenience stores, and made a killing.

Señor Diego Mandito had plenty of cash, more than he knew what to do with, plenty of people, assets, power, and influence, but he still had ambition. How could he turn this mule-hopping business his father started into a legitimate global business? Maybe even get out of the drug game altogether. It was ruthless and very dangerous, with many enemies lining up to take him down.

He had made some investments in mining and minerals, but none had gotten off and been profitable yet.

He had investigated oil in the Gulf of Mexico, but permitting was very strict, controlled, and limited. Despite his billions, it was impossible for anyone but the global exploration companies to break into it. But liquid gold very much appealed to his ambitions.

Although wealthier than most imagined, Mandito wanted more. His roots were humble, but he was driven by the fear of failure. He was Mexican, and in days gone by, he would not have been taken seriously at the business table. He was still paranoid about that, although times had changed.

That's why he had reached out to Lord Beecham and his sidekick, Colonel Collins. They were perfect for helping him legitimize the face of his business, his international business aspirations, and one deal in particular.

Casa Panorama was all set up, staff ready, security in place (as always), and plenty of food and drink to make the best basis of conversation and for them to accept his business proposition. *Why wouldn't they? Who would dare?* he thought and broke into laughter.

Mandito heard his security detail busying themselves as Beecham and Collins arrived at the front gate of the villa, almost a mile away on their approach up the olive-tree-lined, grand entrance. He was looking forward to this meeting. He was looking forward to recruiting these two on his continued journey of business legitimization.

PART III

WHO DARES

IO
CREDIBLE FORCE

February 2019
Hosingow Compound
Somalia, East Africa
7:00 a.m.

BORIS LATMINKO, SENIOR COLONEL OF the Russian
Special Forces sabre squadrons, Spetnaz, sat at the front of
the command tent, watching the progress of the Land Rover
110 as it made its way down from the B9 across the desert,
a plume of dust rising behind as it traversed the rugged
cutout. The vehicle was approaching Latminko's temporary
base of operations. Nairobi was five hundred miles to the
west, and the base was thirty miles south of Hosingow and
equidistant from Kolbio on the Somalian-Kenyan border.
A natural valley of largely plantless terrain, surrounded by
scrub and just a handful of candelabra trees, broke up the
terrain. There was an airstrip engineered from the barren
desert, with three HC-130 aircraft, a collection of sand-swept

tents, and a variety of armored vehicles, weaponry, and equipment. As Latminko well knew, the operation had to fly totally under the radar. Even the uniforms they wore bore no indication of country or rank.

As the vehicle drew closer, it attracted more attention as the occupants of the camp manned their weapons to welcome their visitor.

For what seemed an age in a landscape where not much happens at all, the brown and dusty Land Rover headed up the side of the airstrip and broke camp, pulling up to a halt outside the command tent and Latminko, the focal point of the encampment.

The passenger, with his dark eyes, almost black, and his olive skin, stepped out of the 110, stretched, and took in the scene around him. Latminko, one of two very big men dressed in desert combats, boots, bright-colored *ghutras* wrapped around their necks, ready for the next sandstorm, greeted their guest with steely eyes and grunts, barely looking up from their chess game as their visitor arrived.

The visitor attracted the gaze of the men at the camp, the intensity of the various weapons pointed at him from afar. Even for a friendly visitor, one false move could end up quite badly to say the least, an intimidatory atmosphere created by Latminko, all part of the Spetnaz methodology: use every possible angle to intimidate and defeat your enemy, or even those who are not part of your inner, most trusted circle. In any event, they were on a mission with very high stakes.

"Dobroye utro tovarishchi." The visitor said, "Good morning, comrades," in an accent that wasn't of Russian origin.

The two looked at him for the first time. "Utro tebe tozhe moy drug," Latminko, the bigger of the two very big men, responded in his native Russian tongue and cast a smile. "Morning to you too."

"What do we owe this pleasure?" said Latminko, knowing full well the purpose of the visit.

"I was in Malindi, and I thought I'd pop by to see how plans were progressing," he said as he motioned to the camp, casual about his six-hundred-mile trip across some of the most inhospitable terrain on this most inhospitable continent known as Africa. It was clear that the passenger was no wuss; he had experience dealing with these sorts, and he was used to being in this type of company, but these were no ordinary men at the camp today. These were Russia's finest and most elite soldiers—serving soldiers, despite their lack of insignia.

Latminko eyed his visitor. Tall, slim, fit, muscular but wiry, not a bodybuilder, more of a runner, he thought. He was dressed in hugging jeans, a beige jacket, desert boots, a ghutra of his own, blue on white, and a pair of wraparound sunglasses. It was clear that this man was used to this terrain, probably ex-military and, judging by his accent, of French origin, and by his stance, likely former Foreign Legion, a Legionnaire.

The two big Russians, with bulging biceps and their Russian-issue Grach pistols strapped to their waists, stood up together and held out their hands. They shook and gave a half hug and a slap on the back.

Their visitor was there to check on their progress and readiness to deploy and to see that his paymasters' investments were being used wisely. Latminko knew that the man had an ax to grind with the West, particularly with a certain arm of the British Army, the SAS to be specific. Years ago, according to rumor, a surgical strike killed the visitor's parents, and now he was out for blood, and, by the looks of it, he was about to get what he wanted.

After a couple of hours of briefing, then inspecting the men and their equipment, followed by a night of vodka and song, in midmorning the next day, the Land Rover 110 left the way it had come, disappearing in a plume of dust as it headed back to the B9 and on to the A2, this time back to Nairobi, and from there back to his current home, Malabo, Equatorial Guinea.

11
OLD HAUNTS

Heathrow Airport
London, United Kingdom
3:55 p.m.

MITCH TOUCHED DOWN ON THE British Airways 168 flight direct from Shanghai to London Heathrow. As they taxied to the terminal, Mitch turned on his phone, and after finding the signal to Vodafone UK, the texts, emails, and voice mails downloaded.

Missed calls and a voice mail from a 01432 number caught his attention, Hereford, and a text from the same number, Sam, "Call me now."

As soon as Mitch got into terminal 4, he made his way to the British Airways Flagship Lounge and headed to the quiet area to make his call. He punched the number, listened to the connection, and within three rings heard the familiar voice.

"What the hell were you doing in Moscow, Mitch?" Sam came straight at him, no pleasantries, no discussion, and no introduction. "You were always the rogue, and you know that this is simply not how we work nowadays, Mitch."

Mitch patiently listened as Sam got it off his chest.

"Do you realize the whole world of shit you are in right now?"

Mitch took a sip of his coffee, then quietly and calmly said, "Hey, Sam, good to hear from you. How are you doing? What the fuck are you talking about?"

Mitch could almost hear the former Regimental sergeant major of the most elite force in the world, 22 Special Air Service blow a gasket.

"Mitch, you can fuck about with me all you want and play the lone wolf, but when I get a call from the big white hallways of Pall Mall and word that you, yes you, Mitch, have seriously pissed off arguably the most powerful man in the world, then that is a problem. Wouldn't you fucking say?"

"Who do you mean, Sam? Donald fucking Trump?"

"Fuck off, Mitch. You know exactly who I am talking about, and you know exactly who I am referred to—Bokov and Dankov. Thing is the former is dead to tell no lies, and the latter has woken up from his fucking IED-induced coma to tell it how it is, and photographs of you and Yee are floating around, putting you exactly at the scene of the crime on the right day, the right moment, and the right fucking minute! Mitch, why the fuck didn't you tell me? I could have protected you, laid a smokescreen. You know the fucking drill. What the fuck, Mitch?"

Despite all his years with Sam, Mitch had never heard him swear so much, the son of a schoolteacher and all! He would never take a dressing down from anyone in the same way, but this was Sam, one of his brothers.

"Sam, calm the fuck down before you spin into a fucking seizure."

"Mitch, you have Dankov's boss and arguably the most powerful man in the world on your case, and your name is on top of his fucking hit list! Well fucking done, Mitch. You just hit the fucking jackpot!"

"Sam, trust me. I will be fine. Let's work through this and get to the other side."

"Mitch, we already have sightings of FSB operatives in Marin County, Tiburon, and right on your fucking doorstep in London. Yee has already been taken out, long-range sniper assassination at his hideaway in China."

Mitch went quiet as the weight of the words fell upon him. He knew that at least Bella was safe this time, on her way to meet him in London. His thoughts turned to Angela, in Marin County, on her own, exposed.

"Sam, lets meet up and talk it through. You in Hereford?"

"I could drive down and see you in the morning."

"Yep, let's do that. Usual place?"

"Yep. See you by ten."

"Love you, man."

"Love you too, Mitch. Silly old fucker!"

"If the hat fits, wear it!" responded Mitch, injecting some humor to the conversation.

Sam just responded, "See you tomorrow," and ended the call.

Mitch leaned back in his leather armchair, looked around at all the business passengers passing through, thought about his life, and said, "For fuck's sake!"

He texted both Bella and Angela. "Code check?"

Within a few moments, they both texted back various states of *green*.

"Aren't you due some rest time?" Mitch texted back.

"Seriously?"

"Yep."

"Okay" came the response from Angela three minutes later, as she had absorbed his coded message to *get out of Dodge* and make a tactical retreat to their secret bolt hole. They had put their escape plan in place after Bella had been kidnapped those years ago, somewhere only they knew.

Mitch could feel the annoyance in the text messages. They had been through thick and thin together. Mitch knew his absences had put distance between them over time. He had grown used to that, if not preferring his own company to the company of others. It wasn't that Mitch didn't love Angela, because he did, and there was no other woman in Mitch's life; they had just grown apart, and maybe sometime in Hawaii together might just be the ticket, he thought.

"That would be nice," he said to himself, remembering the fun times they had over the years in the condo, on the island, the brothers-in-law wedding, a jaunt up the volcano, surfing, relaxing by the beach. *As close to paradise as it gets*, he thought, navigating the terminal and immigration.

Only a former soldier could understand the mind-set. The sacrifices he had made for queen and country had taken a toll on him, taking and assuming responsibility for the welfare and sometimes the lives of others, that sense of responsibility, that sense of sacrifice, being willing to put his life on the line for others. That sense of responsibility and ultimate accountability had transgressed into his life as a civilian, and his distancing, an act, was as much to protect others, loved ones, as himself. He knew from experience that people who got close to him had a bad habit of dying on him. He wanted to avoid it at all costs as far as Angela and Bella were concerned. After all these years, they both understood this, silently, always avoiding the topic of conversation. It was an unstated fact of their lives.

Somewhere over the Atlantic Ocean
British Airways Flight 292
Washington Dulles to London Heathrow

Bella sat bolt upright, sweat pouring from her brow, somewhere over the middle of the Atlantic. She had boarded late the night before, gotten delayed on the tarmac, enjoyed a couple of business class gin and tonics, eaten her business class meal, drank a glass or two of the California Merlot from MacRostie Estates, reclined her business class chair into a lie-flat bed, and taken a nap so she was fresh in the morning for her arrival in London.

The memories were still fresh and painful. Her mind went back to apartment 1b, Bromley Hight Street, more than two years ago.

As Mac arrived, second on the scene at 1b, she was uncontrollably sobbing, holding Nikita's body, finding it impossible to deal with the guilt that she should have seen the impossible situation he was in.

She should have—could have—helped him. "My poor Nikita," she said at 37,000 feet above the Atlantic.

The senior British Airways stewardess Joanne spotted that Bella was awake and walked over to her, offering a smile and a drink, seeming to understand Bella's pain. "A cup of tea would be super. English breakfast. Milk, no sugar." She smiled back at the friendly stewardess.

Bella stared out the window into the black, and the memories and the many unanswered questions flooded back.

After she had gotten back to Tiburon, after Mitch had returned home that Christmas, she and her father and mother had probably the most complete time ever as a family. Alone, together, happy in their own company. Cooking at home, laughing, playing cards, playing Trivial Pursuit and board games, taking a walk down at Blackie's Pasture, having breakfast at their favorite place, the Morningside Café, drinks at the Farm Shop—it was what she had always dreamed of as a child, but Mitch was always too busy, always away in some distant land, coming home with exotic gifts.

Nikita's passing was a big blow to Bella. He was the brother she never had. Their connection was much greater than just friends, yet they had never crossed that boundary, although she knew she was—and was sure he was—tempted on more than one occasion. That would have ruined it all.

Jo, the air stewardess, bought her the cup of English breakfast with milk. "Thank you very much." She smiled, enjoying the opportunity to use her queen's English, proper

English. She turned back to her thoughts and the dark window.

Her life had changed dramatically over the last two years or so. Living in the DC area was cool. She enjoyed it—warm and sticky in the summer, cold in the winter, four seasons, relatively drama-free downtown, venturing into the suburbs and not attracting attention. She reminded herself that it was the same in any major city. *Right?* She had grown to enjoy Washington as home, almost as much as she enjoyed Marin, but without the memories, some of them sad.

She had met Wills about a year ago at a joint briefing summit. Wills was working for British Intelligence. He was an army officer, an Imperial College graduate, as bright as a button. He was respectfully shy, a gentleman who dressed like one, with a killer British accent, much better than her own, which had the rounded edges of growing up in California. Nevertheless, she was heading to London and enjoyed immersing herself in her mother tongue.

Finishing her tea, she realized that the next few days might be unpredictable, so she reclined and snuggled up for another couple of hours

Hopefully no more bad dreams. At least for tonight.

To Hereford, England
5:00 a.m.

Mitch jumped in his Audi A6 hire car and took the A40 out of London, joining the M40 past Oxford, then up to Redditch, a short hop down the M5, off at Junction 7, skirt around Worcester, and on to the A4103 into Hereford.

It had been a long while since Mitch made this trip, and as he did, many memories came flooding back.

At Worcester, he decided to take a detour through Tenbury Wells, thirty minutes north of Hereford, and track the same route he had taken all those years ago with his mother and father as they dropped him at the gates of Stirling Lines when he showed up for his tour of duty with the Special Air Service.

A lifetime ago, he thought as he pushed the supercharged four-wheel drive Audi.

As the miles passed by, the memories mounted.

Mitch recalled his first call of duty in Northern Ireland with the Regiment and how he landed alone at Belfast City Airport and was picked up by his handler and bundled into the back of a Ford Transit van. He used his holdall for padding on the flat bed in the rear of the van, as there were no seats. He was unceremoniously dropped off at his new home, the Big Green Barn at Aldergrove International Airport, to meet his new team.

The ranges in Hereford with their army-issue raincoats and Heckler & Koch MP5s being drawn from their holsters. The "Why did you only put thirty-eight rounds into them?" question and the "My magazine ran out" answer. He remembered Gonzo, Lawrence, Dinger, Red, Tom, and Vince. He remembered Sam, Bob, Ryan, and Mac. He remembered the Paludrine Club, the Gamecock at the back of Stirling Lines. He remembered the Sunday sips and farewells before dispatch to unkown territoires on Monday morning, the ubiquitous "Have a good trip," never knowing if you would see your brother-in-arms ever again.

It was an honor to serve with the Regiment, albeit an existence of uncertainty, the unkown, adaptability being high on the traits needed to survive, or as Mitch recalled how one of his mates put it, buoyancy.

Mitch got to the Sawley Arms and turned left onto the A456, past the Temeside Inn and on the drop down to Tenbury Wells High Street.

He drove down the lane to Cadmore Lodge, now a retirement home, and paused for a moment, looking at the lake, remembering a wedding many years in his past—Christine, Jean, Alan, and their family. He spun the Audi around on the gravel, creating a crunch, and headed back into Tenbury. He popped into the Rose & Crown for a Farmers Half and then headed on to meet Sam at the Vaults in Hereford.

As he sped out of the little market town, he was glad to leave behind the memories and the same feeling he had had all those years ago around fleeing the trap of middle-class life in a forgotten town—beautiful and friendly but in the middle of nowhere, and apart from the resident soda factory, with little or no prospects for its inhabitants of whatever age.

He headed south on the A49, toward Hereford, and turned on the radio.

"I've been down on bended knee talkin' to the man from Galilee. He spoke to me in the voice so sweet. I thought I heard the shuffle of the angel's feet."

Twenty minutes later as he headed into Hereford, he passed the Starting Gate, where he had met Angela all those years ago with Jimmy. She had been through so much. He had put her there, and the demons of her past had helped.

Jimmy was gone. Long gone now. "Poor bastard," Mitch said to himself.

And then there was Sam. Twenty-five years in the army. Eighteen of those with the Regiment. Retirement. Sheep, flowers, and governor's meetings. Wife dead, book on the way. "What the fuck?" Mitch said aloud.

Which is the better path? To live long or die happy? Mitch found himself pondering that question in his mind once again. "Now that is the fucking question."

He pulled up outside of the Vaults and couldn't quite work out what was wrong with him. Was he angry? Was it that he had seen too much? Was it that he simply didn't care anymore?

He had come to a similar conclusion years ago when his father died before him.

At his age, with his level of experience and the old soldier mentality, Mitch was scared of no one, and the apparent threat from Dankov didn't bother him too much. In fact, he sort of relished it, the constant threat to keep him on his toes and prevent the smoking jacket and slippers. He did have to admit he was rather surprised that Dankov survived the bomb blast. A matter of good luck for Dankov and bad luck for him. The assassination of Yee, the Dog, came as a blow as well. Well, life was full of twists and turns. He just had to accept that he wasn't done with the Russians. Not by a longshot.

Fighting the fight is what he'd done since a boy, since eleven years old, taking up boxing, fighting off the threats, protecting others, until he grew to enjoy it, to get a buzz, not so much that he would ever provoke unnecessarily but always a finisher with that bittersweet sense of victory afterward. "How dare you fuck with me"—the ancestral cry.

Sam was an old friend, a good friend, and in years gone by wouldn't give a fuck about the Dankov threat, would probably feel the same as Mitch about the situation, but Sam was being sensitive. He had gone from top job to Regimental alumnus, from happily married to now a widower, and from gung ho to *What the fuck next?*

Sam needed more help than Mitch. That was for sure.

Mitch parked the Audi, headed to the Lichfield Vaults, and just as he was walking through the door to the bar, said louder than probably needed, "Fuck you, Dankov!"

The same old collection of local alcoholics were having their midday pick-me-up, a few big-timers, businessmen with expensive suits and little wallets, and there was Sam, sitting in the back room, in jeans, a dress shirt, and sports jacket, with a small veteran's badge on his lapel.

Mitch realized his place and misplace in this world and how moving back in time wasn't healthy. He needed to march on. *One sure foot in front of the other,* as his father had always taught him.

5 Eaton Square, Belgravia
London, United Kingdom
10:00 a.m.

Mac got a cab straight from the airport to check out his property. It had been a while since he had been there, and last time, he was cleaning up the carnage of his former wife, Viktoria, who had been dispatched in the most ruthless of fashion. In exchange for her crime, treason, she bled to death with her eyes gouged out. That was the punishment, Rastrojos style.

The last thing he did before leaving London last time was pose as a window cleaner and place a very inconspicuous camera under the eaves of the building across the road. When the unit was not broadcasting, which was most of the time, it was impossible to detect.

All Mac was aiming to do was understand the level of interest in this asset that, as a result of his ex-wife's demise, was now his by rights of marriage and being the sole beneficiary of her will.

With a current property market value in excess of $15 million, and the value of art, paintings, antiques, and furniture within probably worth the same again, this was Mac's chance to buy his dream and more in what was home to him now, Chile.

He and a young Nikita, on the way back from a coastal visit to Valparaiso, had come across a vineyard that was remote, beautiful, and the perfect paradise. If Mac sold this place in Belgravia, and all its lavish contents, he could buy the villa in Chile, boost the wine business, and live happily ever after, which had long been his hope.

Mac circled the property, first in the car, driving around three times, then on foot. He checked it out, every detail, until he concluded there was no evidence of tampering, which was a double confirmation of the data from the camera across the street. There was only the daily trudge of the mailman to the front door. Thankfully, the professional mailbox automatically dispatched, sorted, and stored the mail, a precaution that Viktoria had taken, given her busy lifestyle and long periods away from home, in addition to the risk her job entailed.

The fundamental fish wires and tags that Mac had laid still remained and further confirmed that no one had been to the place since he left.

As he cracked the solid front door, he disarmed the alarm, and he could smell the pungency of the chemicals used for the cleanup that bloody day.

He realized that no one was paying attention to this property or its contents. He called his old friend Tonja Brodie, a Kiwi, a South African of immense beauty and charm and a raving nymphomaniac to boot, at least in her time. With her blonde, short hair, ski jump cute nose, tight derriere, and love of sex, Mac and Tonja had enjoyed their carnal pleasures many times, mostly starting at the Coogee Bay Hotel in Sydney, which he had frequented for a while at one point in his life.

Tonja was now in London, married with kids but still as hot as ever. Mac wondered if she still shared the pleasures in bed with her husband today as she once did with him.

Never mind. Today was about cashing out. Tonja worked for Sotheby's, and he wanted to engage her to sell the estate—the property and its contents. Get it on the market, the London, Belgravia market, sell it quickly, get the price, extract the cash, and go.

The contents of the property might take a little longer, but there was an auction coming up in two weeks that could fit the bill.

Mac wanted to rid, sell up, release his money, and make investments elsewhere, including Villa Valparaiso, the name he had decided on for his new home in Chile. Carmen would be over the moon, he thought as he mulled this fantasy, so close to making it a reality.

Viktoria had been a hard woman. Mac fell in love with her long legs, blue eyes, and at one point her insatiable need for sex. They both wanted it and needed it at the time. He quickly fell out of love with her unwavering need to control every aspect of theirs and other people's lives, behaving like a god that makes decisions on the part of others and changes life's natural process.

She rose to fame when she joined the Lithuanian National Party and protested the corruption that existed. She and others knew that in order to join the European Union, corruption had to be eliminated, at least from common view.

One of her first victories was stopping the equivalent of GroMart in Lithuania winning the rights to build and operate the country's first nuclear power station.

Her political aspirations grew as she saw an opportunity to get closer to the Kremlin and her deep ancestral connection to the motherland, Russia, and to be the next queen of the Russian Federation.

Then she met Dmitri Dankov, and her perspective and career progression changed.

Mac looked at the Amber Room and thought of how he still despised Viktoria today. He just wanted to cash out and buy his Villa Valparaiso. In it, he would have a dedication to Nikita, his son.

12
OLD FRIENDS

August 2018
Palace of the Tsars, Shores of the Black Sea
Sochi, Russian Federation
9:00 a.m.

ELEGANTLY AND BRAZENLY SITTING ABOVE the Black Sea, nestled in ancient forest and highly secretive, the Palace of the Tsars resembled the Palace of Versailles or some other monument of power, wealth, and greatness. The irony was that it was owned by the leading communist leader of the world. *Communism for the people, apart from those who deserve wealth and power the most*, Dankov often reminded himself, trying to stay true to own father's teachings.

Dankov's thoughts were interrupted by the ring of a bell in the distance, signaling time for breakfast. Dankov climbed out of bed and strapped his new prosthetic leg around his waist, slipping into the harness and flicking the switch to enable its state-of-the-art robotic features to work their magic.

His visitor at the Petrovskie Voroto Hospital that day had kept his word and ensured that the best medical attention and care were afforded to this patriot of the motherland. Dankov was grateful that his father's old friend from college, now president of Russia, had taken him under his wing all those years ago. His father had disappeared under mysterious circumstances, and Putin had stepped in. Now, it seemed, Dankov owed Putin everything, and he wouldn't forget it.

Although his recovery, his treatment, and his acclimatization to his new limb were going well, he sat back into his wheelchair and maneuvered it to the breakfast room of his apartment, lost in this grand palace, overlooking the resplendent grounds and the Black Sea shore.

The impeccable blonde, the delightful breakfast hostess, served his breakfast of scrambled eggs, smoked salmon, capers, grapefruit juice, and coffee. Alongside were copies of the *Moscow, London,* and *New York Times.*

He pulled up his wheelchair to his daily routine, realizing that he was adjusting nicely to his new existence.

He remembered nothing from the actual explosion or the immediate time before or after. Luckily for Dankov, he had been thrown through the door from the blast but had still experienced life-changing injuries. Losing his leg from the groin was the biggest physical trauma. His broken arm had healed and was getting stronger with the weights, but the scars from the burns down his right side and on his face were visible and would never go away.

He carried the scars, the memories, and an intense desire for revenge. One of the objects of his rage, Yee, the Dog, had already been taken out. But there were more targets on the list, specifically Mitch, his wife, and his daughter.

His phone buzzed, and he took his last forkful of scrambled eggs, then a sip of coffee. He stood up slowly from his wheelchair and slowly but purposefully limped to the balcony overlooking the forest and the shoreline. He put the phone to his ear.

"Privet."

"Rabota vypolnena?" Job done?

"Da. Vavsgeda?" Yes. Job done.

"Zhena I doch?" Wife and daughter?

"Gone."

"Good work, comrade."

The phone went dead.

Dankov walked back into his daily routine—private nurse, exercise, and road to recovery. "Takes more than big bomb to take Dankov." He smiled as the rather voluptuous, attractive, and accommodating nurse went down before him.

August 2018
Langley
Virginia, United States
6:00 p.m.

Bella sat in her apartment in Langley poring over the materials for her final CIA examinations. She had been singled out for her expertise and focus on geopolitical analysis. As part of that, she had been given Africa to study.

She could have made a call to her friends at Executive Outcomes but wanted to be seen doing the grunt work and come up with her own conclusions. Sure, she could draw on her previous intel, but she didn't want to reach out again, not now. It would have felt like she was cheating, and that just wasn't right.

Africa had long been thought of as the undiscovered continent with all its wealth of resources, minerals discovered and not, and its base population. Organizing, settling, and aligning these resources must surely remain the last opportunity in the six-continent power play. North and South America were tied up, as was Europe, apart from the Russia thing. Asia and Australasia were in political battles for rights in the North and South Poles, and even Trump was making a play to acquire Greenland to expand the US territories.

Apart from the inevitable and growing bartering and bantering around the poles, the extraterrestrial battle was starting to heat up. But in the meantime, Africa still remained the biggest opportunity, with China and Russia taking number one and number two spots in their success in laying long-term investments and long-term bets.

She went back over her paper again. It was a good summary of the history over the last two hundred years and more recently how specific investments and political alignments, largely with the Chinese and Russian governments, were signals now for longer-term concern—specifically, investments in infrastructure projects, roads, bridges, airports, and so on. Long-term investments and returns over twenty, thirty, fifty, and a hundred years were further signals.

Telephony and communication exchanges. Mobile phone networks. Internet enablement of previously unserved populations. Creating better access—or, in most cases, for the very first time—to the internet, creating connectivity, eventual transaction revenue the obvious allure.

But for China and Russia, this was an opportunity to court and conquer land mass outside their own borders and gain access to the potential future workforce, minerals, and riches that existed in the largest continent at the center of the world.

A big bet. A potentially very big prize.

She remembered her father's saying about Northern Ireland. The same applied to Africa. "Anyone who says that they understand Africa doesn't really understand Africa." She smiled at Wills, who was patiently waiting for her to finish her work. *That's Africa, Baby! (TAB)*: although not quite the heading of an orthodox CIA report, Bella wasn't orthodox, and she was tempted to use that for the title anyway.

On the buildup to and during the Arab Spring, it had become obvious that new weapons of war were now in play. Social media was the new tool that could be used to unsettle nations and leaders, influence elections and population rising. This was the same way that the Russians and others had influenced the US presidential elections, and it was just the tip of the iceberg. These tactics had been deployed for decades; social media was just the new medium.

Bella remembered her father lamenting how Russia had made the first funding available to the IRA to get them off the ground. How the Germans during World War I had armed the Irish and fueled their revolt against the English to add to their woes from the führer, and how over decades the stupid Americans had succumbed to the propaganda of the struggles from the old country and funded the most heinous form of crime, greed, and terrorism, not on their soil but that of Northern Ireland and Britain.

The power of this medium and its ability to turn people against governments and subject them to the power of propaganda was more potent than ever before. Information is power, and the control of information was yet more powerful still.

Bella, tapping away at her Apple Mac Pro was finalizing her paper and her responses in preparation for tomorrow's final exam.

She had long completed her boot camp at Camp Peary, or the Farm, near Williamsburg, Virginia. This was her final hurdle.

She looked over to Wills, smiled, and raised her glass of MacRostie Pinot Noir. Then she kissed him on the lips. Patiently and with loving eyes, he smiled, kissing Bella back—not just a kiss but one that let her know that he understood, he was okay with her dedication, and he loved her right back, if not more so.

Wills was originally from the UK, a little town just outside of Hereford where his mother had met his father, who was serving with the Special Air Service at the time. His parents had a tumultuous marriage, separating by the time he was eighteen months old and ever since managed to enjoy the privilege of hating and hurting each other. Their lives were so intertwined and reflections of each other. *Maybe they were too much like each other.* That was why Bella had a nagging doubt that they were too similar to be together, at least forever.

Eventually, it came down to money. His father wanted a relationship. Wills and his mother just wanted the money, and then his grandmother stepped in the way of providing the money and replacing the father. Wills had not spoken to his father for ten years despite the odd message, birthday card, and Christmas card. Grandmother's payoff had seen to any future contact. At least for now.

He had met Bella while in Washington, DC, with the British Foreign Office. They both worked in the same area of expertise—understanding world geopolitical threats and opportunities.

The whole Operation Argus debacle was legendary. Nikita Saparov's mercurial insights and the billions of dollars he had made for others as a result, despite his demise, had made him a hero, an icon of this very specialized group of people and profession.

Wills raised his glass to Bella. They clinked and kissed once more. She wondered if this was it. Maybe someday. They spent more quiet time together while she completed her paper, and then they went to bed and made love.

As they rolled over from each other's passion, Wills whispered in Bella's ear as she fell asleep, "Good luck tomorrow, Bella." He thought about that for a second and followed up. "As if you need it, my Bella, Bella Fonterella." Words that were too familiar to Bella. Words that had been with her since she was a child.

"Good night, Bella."

13
INSIDER TRADING

March 2019
Ingram, High-Security Satellite
Cabo San Lucas, Baja California, Mexico
7:58 a.m.

"HELLO, THANK YOU FOR JOINING the Ingram high-security call. Your conference call will start momentarily. Hello, thank you for joining the Ingram high-security call. Your conference call will start momentarily. Hello, thank you for joining the Ingram high-security call. Your conference call will start momentarily. Hello, thank you for joining the Ingram high-security call. Your conference call will start momentarily ..."

The hold music resembled elevator music in a cheap Moscow hotel, and the automated message from the female voice with a canned Californian accent was enough to annoy the most patient of people, never mind Señor Diego Mandito. He sipped a cool drink in his Casa Panorama on the cliff overlooking the Pacific Ocean, eyeing the cell on the table next to the glass. The phone was on speaker, and the canned voice of an operator kept telling him his call was important. He sighed, shook his head, and wondered what the world was coming to.

The irony of the thought wasn't lost on him when he considered what he did to earn his handsome fortune. His home represented much more than the fruits of his labors. It symbolized an understanding among him and his competitors. Cabo San Lucas was a relatively safe place to be, as the cartels had consistently honored their pacts in the spirit of protecting and preserving the tourist business, but nowadays, they trusted one another more than the government, who had become focused and aggressive in tackling the cartels. That was why he wanted out. That was why he had entertained the approach from the Russians via his friends in Cuba, and that was why he had sent $500 million to his new comrades in Moscow to seal the deal.

As he continued to hold and look at the ocean, he heard the voice on the end of the conference line, via a satellite phone that the Russians had given him—100 percent secure.

He was two minutes early for the call, maybe another indication of how he and his culture were different from the people he was dealing with. He trusted no one at the best of times, and his paranoia was growing, seeing that Russians were no different from anyone else.

That said, he knew it was time to slide out of the drug business. He had already made his billions. He had legitimate business interests in Mexico, but this was his chance to expand globally and get out of this rat race that was becoming too crowded, too dangerous, and a too-high-risk venture.

To divert some of his wealth from ill-gotten gains and take control and a partial share of Africa's sixth-largest oil-producing nation, with more than 317,000 barrels a day, sounded like a good escape plan. He knew that jumping in bed with unlikely partners was a risk, but he couldn't take his eyes off the play from turning dirty money to clean, and even at forty dollars a barrel, there was $12.5 million a day spewing out of the ground in Equatorial Guinea.

The deal was that he would just take a sleeping partner role in the arrangement. He would fund the crew, the operation, and the coup, and his bed partners would then take over and assume control, and he would just take the royalties for his efforts—a cool $500 million a year, ad infinitum. That was even better than Michael Jordan's infamous deal with Nike! He laughed at himself, despite being pissed off with listening to the autonomon voice on the phone. He was not used to waiting for anyone—ever.

"Hello, thank you for joining the Ingram high-security call. Your conference call will start momentarily."

Mandito looked out to the ocean and noticed something he had never seen before, what looked like a military naval vessel. He had read about the ARM *Durango*, a new ship in the Mexican fleet, sailing along the shore, no whales, a Mexican flag ahoy and its SA-18 Grouse missiles pointing right at Casa Panorama.

"Hello, thank you for joining the Ingram high-security call. Your conference call will start momentarily."

He looked at the *Durango*, looked at the satellite phone the Russians gave him, then looked around at his staff before turning and seeing the flare of the SA-18's launch that within milliseconds would destroy Casa Panorama. "Malditos enganosos bastardos." (You cheating, fucking bastards.)

The satellite phone repeated, "Hello, thank you for joining the Ingram high-security call. Your conference call will start momentarily." Maybe no one was going to join after all.

The first of the series of missiles hit Casa Panorama. Mandito could feel the whole building shake like in some mega earthquake, taking out the entire west wing of the villa, glass smashing, debris and dust flying, and the sheer, unimaginable heat vaporizing all in its path and sending a blistering wind of destruction. Time slowed down. Mandito could see his life before him. Mandito was on his hands and knees, covering his ears from the horrifying and disorientating sound wave of the first blast. Within seconds, the second and third missiles hit, wiping Mandito's palatial villa off the top of the cliff, vaporizing all that was there, and everything went black.

The three plumes of smoke arose from what rubble remained, and within a few hours, a small army of excavation vehicles and construction workers would make their way up the olive-tree-lined driveway to the now vacant plot, building a replacement villa, equally if not more luxurious as the previous one but certainly more secure. The new villa would be called Casa Blanca.

Somewhere among what remained came a sound, a female autonomon, "Welcome to Ingram High Security.

Your conference call has now been canceled. Thank you and goodbye."

This would be reported in the local news as a domestic gas explosion, and the media would quickly and hastily move on to other more newsworthy matters.

The Union Club
Greek Street, London, United Kingdom
11:00 a.m.

Lord Beecham and Colonel Collins stepped into the town car, with James behind the wheel, from the gate of Beecham's pad in Chelsea. They were heading to Greek Street and the big red door otherwise known as the Union Club, a twenty-minute ride given the traffic today.

The sleek black Range Rover with black leather seats and supercharged 5.0-liter engine was silent in the back as they both gazed out the window, London passing by before them. They passed the Natural History Museum, the V&A, then Harrods, Wellington Arch, Buckingham Palace, the National Gallery, the Theater District, the West End, and Soho before reaching Greek Street.

Beecham was deep in thought. After their meeting with Mandito and his attempt at recruiting his services to help him take over Equatorial Guinea and its black gold, he had received the news that Casa Panorama and Mandito were no longer. He found it difficult to believe that he had been there with Mandito just a week earlier. And the brutality of his disposal was shocking.

He of course knew of Bianca Blanca, and her reputation preceded her—smart, political, savvy, and clearly ruthless—but he also recognized the way of the jungle, the Mexican jungle. Then when you add in the cutthroat nature of the cartels and their business, the sheer volume of money slushing around, the power struggles, and the greed, justifying the events became somewhat more understandable but nevertheless incomprehensible.

These were unprecedented times though. He continued with his thoughts as he got ready to brief the rest of the crew. Never before had such a complex plot of unlikely collaborators been hatched, with an equally unlikely target and objective.

As Beecham put the pieces together though, the plot made sense; in fact, he credited it with "Absolute bloody genius."

As the car entered Soho and drew closer to the Union, Beecham turned his thoughts to the task at hand, and that was primarily to protect Mitch and his daughter, Bella. They were in grave danger, with a contract on their heads, authorized by the Kremlin and at the hands of probably the most ruthless and powerful dark army anywhere in the world—the Russian Mafia.

They had been here many times before. Double tap on the big red door, and the Union welcomed them back to their humble and eclectic home. Michaela greeted them at the front reception, a small hallway with stairs rising behind, leading to the private dining room and meeting rooms, and to the right, through a door to the bar, dining room, and lounge.

"Good morning, Lord Beecham," Michaela said with a warm and welcoming smile. "Colonel Collins, it's been a while," she said.

"Michaela, my darling," Beecham said, and he gave her a double kiss on each cheek and a passing embrace. Collins offered the same.

"Michaela, how've you been, my darling?" Beecham said as she escorted them into the downstairs bar.

Beecham spotted some familiar faces and regulars at the Union. Tim, Keith, and Ernie were having coffee and what looked like a very serious morning brief. He recognized Scarlett Johansson having an intimate conversation with someone he assumed was an agent or the director of her next film. Stephen Fry was in an equally engaged conversation with another chap, both in their Uppingham School style, bright colored corduroys, sports jackets complete with elbow patches, open-neck shirts and cravats. *Very bohemian*, Beecham thought.

Beecham and Collins joined Tim, Keith, and Ernie and ordered their lattes. When Michaela had left, Tim said, "What the hell is going on?" with his usual straight-to-the-point tone.

"Is this place secure?" Beecham asked, then received resounding nods.

"No listeners?" Collins asked.

"All clear," responded Tim, looking at Keith, the former Scotland Yard man.

Ernie, in his direct, London, East End style, asked the obvious questions. "Hey, Beecham, what the fuck is going on here? What's all the secrecy? Should we be locking our wives and daughters up?"

Beecham let out a big smile and beamed around the group of his old friends. "You are the best of the best. Cheers!" He raised his latte to them, giving absolutely nothing away. It wasn't that he didn't trust the three, but what he had in his briefcase was best kept under wraps. The more people who knew, the more lives that would be put in peril.

"Nothing we can't handle, boys, but if we need the cavalry, you will be the first I'll call," Beecham said with a wink and a smile.

Beecham and Collins walked through the bar into the depths of the building, through the lounge and the television room, past a door that led up a private stairway to a private room above the back lounge. *A private room in a very private club. Perfect*, Beecham thought.

They were expecting a crowd today, and as they entered the private room, James, Beecham's man, was already busy setting up the audio-visual, the live feed, and the video links.

Lord Beecham kicked off the meeting. The group had been summoned and made their way to the meeting at the Union, on Greek Street in London, from their various locations around the world.

Mitch and Bella sat together, Sam and Mac at the side, Bob on the other side. Just them for now. The audience would be expanded later.

Coffee, tea, and orange juice sat on the side with delicate reception sandwiches and a selection of cakes and pastries, enough to satisfy their hunger from their variously different journeys.

"Thanks, all, for making your way here with such short notice. I really appreciate it," started Beecham. "Mitch, thanks for rallying the troops."

Mitch nodded acknowledgment.

The room quietened as the screens came to life and the grainy pictures of two men appeared on the screen. Mitch recognized them both immediately; one was of himself, and the other was of Conrad Yee, 狗, Gǒu, the Dog, in Russia—Moscow.

Everyone was attentive, wanting to find out why they had been summoned to London.

"These two pictures were presented to us by the Russians earlier this week," Beecham acknowledged and nodded over to Digby at the table. Digby nodded back and sent a smile over to Bella, making eye contact for a moment. Bella held the stare for a second, then glanced back at the screen, blushing ever so slightly. Digby noticed, but no one else did.

"Two men, we all know, after blowing up Dmitri Dankov and Ivan Bokov's black S-Class Mercedes Benz in Moscow."

Next. Another picture appeared on the screen. A man in traditional Chinese robes sat on a chair, eyes wide open above his high cheekbones, a red dot in the middle of his forehead. Yee, the old dog, was now a dead dog.

Beecham continued, "Whoever the assassin was, they just took the scalp of arguably the most feared and secretive contract assassin on the planet."

Lord Beecham paused and looked around the room at his audience, enjoying the drama of his presentation. This was clearly news to Mitch, who suddenly looked more worried than he had been when he arrived in the room.

"Some of you have already seen this photograph from our man in deepest, darkest Chinese territory. It seems that Yee had retired and retreated to the safest haven that he knew, on the edge of the South China Sea in a small fishing village, Chengkoucun."

The gravity of what Beecham was saying weighed on the room as eyes flickered to Mitch, who just kept a stone wall, game face, not a blink.

Digby piped up with his Etonian flair. "We believe that the meeting in London with the Russian FSB was just a warning call for one of our own."

He exchanged another glance with Bella.

Beecham turned and looked at Mitch for a long moment, eye to eye. Mitch maintained his game face, and the presentation moved on.

The next footage on the screen was what looked like a Heli-cam of a scene of carnage on a hilltop somewhere exotic. The rubble looked like a building of sorts that had been devastated by a weapon of war. "Maybe a nuclear fucking bomb," Mac offered from the group. The screen pulled up an image of a local Cabo San Lucas newspaper with the headline "Gas Leak Destroys Luxury Villa."

"Just last week, Collins and I were invited to Casa Panorama." Beecham pointed at the screen. "Upon the invitation of one Señor Diego Mandito." Another image appeared of who they all recognized as the most powerful and infamous drug lord of Mexico and Central America.

The audio buzzed to life. "Hello, thank you for joining the Ingram high-security call. Your conference call will start momentarily."

"We know that at the time of the attack, Mandito was on a Russian satellite device for a conference call that never was. We believe he was a target of his own making, the phone pinpointing his whereabouts for the strike."

The participants in the room looked at one another, sharing looks of confusion.

The next images showed satellite images over time and what seemed to be a buildup of equipment and forces. It was Bella's turn. "This is on the Somalian-Kenyan border, East Africa. Over the past three months, there has been a steady assemblance of what can only be described as a small army."

She glanced over Digby's way and continued. "Three HC-130s, a dozen mine-resistant, ambush-protected (MRAP) M-ATVs, two dozen Polaris MRZRs, a dozen Navistar MaxxPros troop carriers, Ground Mobility Vehicles (GMVs), a dozen AM General's Hawkeye Howitzer Systems, around four hundred boots, and an arsenal of small weapons, munitions, mines, and explosives."

"Where the hell are they going?" Bob asked.

"The HC-130s with a range of four thousand miles could take them into the Middle East, up to Europe, or south to South Africa, but we think we have a pretty good idea where they are heading," replied Collins.

"And now we have this," Lord Beecham said. "Bob, I think you'll recognize the voice as that of Hamza Malik." The audio snapped to life, and Bob nodded.

"That's the scumbag. I'd recognize his voice anywhere."

"Confirm contact. Force ready. Due to head out next week," came the crackly message.

Another image popped up on the screen, this time a big man in a Russian military uniform, like a passport photo. Digby took the lead. "This is Boris Latminko, senior colonel of the Russian Special Forces sabre squadrons, Spetnaz. Latminko is leading this small army—no insignia, no ranks, just a group of Russian Special Forces using US military hardware to stage a coup."

Digby paused for dramatical effect.

"A coup in Equatorial Guinea."

"Just like in Crimea," Sam declared.

"Just like the fucking Wonga coup," Bob said.

"Yep. But this time it's different. This isn't just about taking back some old Soviet territory or gaining a port in the Black Sea. This is a move on foreign sovereign soil and one of the largest producers of oil in Africa," Beecham added.

"How the fuck do they think they are going to get away with it?" asked Mac.

Bella took the stage to answer. "Because the Russians have been building up a peace-keeping force in the Democratic Republic of Congo, right next door. So, Boris and his mates stage the coup, topple the existing rule, and the Russians step in to keep the peace and, in a void of power and leadership, take control!"

Beecham and Collins nodded as Bella talked through the scenario, the others shaking their heads in disbelief.

"So, now to the funders and the unlikely group of collaborators," Bella continued.

The screen flipped again to a picture of a group of six West African men dressed in expensive suits, in what looked like an opening ceremony, a ribbon-cutting type event.

"Hey," Bob said, "those guys are the BGPC Six. I had them shanghaied a few years earlier, out of Equatorial Guinea. They were skimming millions. Once we got them back to the UK, we gave them the choice of forking over $150 million or paying the piper in a different way."

"Yes, that's right, Bob. They paid up, and they all returned to Equatorial Guinea within a month, never to return to BGPC."

"What the fuck are these fuckwits doing in this scenario?" asked Bob

Beecham smiled. "This is the Presidential Six. They have helped fund this with a collection of $500 million of their own money and a further $500 million from our Señor Mandito, and they will be the face of Equatorial Guinea post the coup."

"With the Russians pulling the strings," Mac observed.

"And the Mexican dead," commented Sam.

"And, ladies and gentlemen, one Russian who is still very much alive." He showed a long-distance snap of a man in a wheelchair on the balcony of what looked like a palace somewhere. James zoomed in on the man and the scarring to the right side of his face.

"Dmitri fucking Dankov," Mitch said in a voice of amazement.

They all exchanged glances, realizing the implication of this factor alone.

"So, what does all this mean? The Russians, cartels, these East Africans, Dankov?" Sam asked.

"And what the fuck does this have to do with us?" asked Mac.

Digby piped in. "Well, my friends, first, some of us in this room are in grave danger." He looked at Mitch and Bella. "Dankov is after revenge, and he has already taken out Yee. He sent a warning to Bella in the US." The room looked at Bella quizzically.

"And there's more," James said. "While you guys were getting set for the briefing, I noticed that two guys were hanging out outside." He pulled up the CCTV shot from the front of the Union. "And now these two monkeys are on your tail. Russian FSB, Ivan Gorky and Ivan Kozlov seconded to Dankov's dark army three months ago."

"Mitch, what the fuck were you doing in Moscow, playing with bombs?" asked Bob.

"I think that should be pretty obvious by now," Mitch said.

"How do we fit into all this?" Mac asked.

Beecham moved the conversation on quickly. "To answer your question, Mac, because we are the only ones who have figured this out. The value of understanding the outcome of this puzzle is worth a billion dollars at the very least, a localized counterwar, or even a major escalation with Russia itself and the players involved, especially Dmitri Dankov, who's out for revenge, and his master, Vladimir Putin. The stakes are high, the consequences deadly, and the outcomes potentially bloody lethal for all of us and anyone who gets in their way."

"And the implications of knowing also has a value. Look at poor old fucking Señor M in Mexico. With that sort of money and opportunity kicking around, you can even get a fucking Mexican naval ship to fire off a missile or two to eliminate unnecessary and unwanted guests," Mac said.

Lord Beecham could see that the news was taking time to sink in. They sat there staring at the screen and thinking it through. There was a lot to think about.

14
MASKIROVKA

The Kremlin
Moscow, Russian Federation
6:30 a.m.

HE SAT IN HIS BIG wingback chair, in his big marble office looking down upon Red Square. He was an early riser; he liked to catch the worm. With the 2016 US elections done and dusted, the impossible had happened. A political outlier, a billionaire, a reality TV host, and a general showboat had made his way to the White House. *A great source of satisfaction*, he thought as he took a sip of his tea and smiled.

He had been watching the US press closely over the past months—the repercussions, the Mueller inquiry, the nonsensical approach to the investigation. Of course, they were asking the wrong question, too high a bar. The question wasn't if Trump and his buffoons had colluded with the Russians. The real question was if they accepted their efforts in full knowledge of their existence. That was the right question.

"Yeblya Idioty," he said and took another sip of his tea. "Fucking idiots."

After the national shame and humiliation of the breakdown of the Soviet Union, his mission was to win back the pride of his country and return to superpower status, their rightful place at the top of world politics, power, and the wealth now associated with the leader of a Communist Russia.

He was playing a master class of chess, and he was making good ground. He liked that. He took another sip of his tea, smiling to himself.

This was his form of meditation. He would do this each day, maybe a different location, a different view. It was an important part of his modus operandi—to stare at the game board, review all the pieces and positions, plan at least eight moves ahead, keep in front of the enemy and the goal of victory. He liked to do this early in the morning, when far lesser minds were still in bed, snoring off their vodka from the night before, scratching their balls, and dreaming about their next McDonald's. His mind created an image of Donald Trump doing the same.

"Yeblya Idioty."

His own career had flourished from his roots in the KGB and into politics in the Soviet Union and now the Russian Federation. The corridors of power were the perfect classroom to learn these fine and subtle skills. Those who didn't would lose and disappear. He who did would rise to the top, survive, thrive, and rule. That was this man's story.

His last play took out what was arguably one of the most qualified candidates for the post of president in a very long time—a career politician, former First Lady, going on to earn herself some of the most senior positions in government in her own right.

He didn't want her to win. She didn't like him, and he certainly didn't like her—or her husband, who he blamed at least in part, along with Gorbachev and Yeltsin, for selling off the state's crown jewels and creating oligarchs, the rule of the few. At least he had managed to handpick most of those candidates, all of which he knew, some of whom were friends, at least at the time, not any more in some cases.

Most of them kept in line, but the likes of Khodorkovsky, who thought that he was bigger than the state, forgetting that it was he who had made him in the first place, suffered the consequences of disrespect and lack of conformity.

Even though Clinton had won the popular vote, she was disliked by many. Tales of questionable dealings, aspersions on her character, divisive campaigning, and the scandals around Benghazi and the use of her email server fueled the dislike. Trump, meanwhile, with a little help from his friends, had won her opposition—the uneducated, the blue-collar voters, the rural voters—and the electoral college system had failed her. For many, the apparent dislike and lack of trust among women had further damaged her cause, despite winning the most votes across the United States.

So much for the best democracy in the world, he thought, not for the first time. It was a statement of arrogance and a statement of aspiration, as he wanted Russia to be at the top of that tree and topple the Americans back to their rightful place of a nation of immigrants and mediocrity.

Clinton had made it easy for him. And Trump was their boy. He had made it easy too, not expecting to have a credible chance but offering an alternative to the career politicians in a time when the voter had lost trust. Just enough of a crack for the propaganda machine to drive a wedge into those groups of voters, some of them voting for the first time, deflecting their choices away from the traditional to the new. He smiled again at his artful achievements.

It really was one of his better plays. He took another sip of his Earl Grey and a bite of his madeleine cake, looking out the window at the square, as people were appearing in the morning light, walking to work, tourists admiring the architecture, couples holding hands, children playing. A snow flurry started to dust the scene, as it often shows in postcards. This was his picture postcard of his nation's capital and his seat of power.

He had enjoyed all the rumors of collusion when, apart from a couple of potential property deals in years gone by, there was none. Granted, there was the sharing of leaked information, but frankly, this would have made it into the public domain without their greasing the wheels. It maybe expedited its release by a few weeks.

The Mueller investigation was highly amusing to him and had rolled on about apparent clandestine meetings about Trump Towers in Moscow. His election team's connections with people allegedly close to the Kremlin, the arrests, the charges, and the incarcerations had all added fuel to the fire of the story and created doubt—claims that he hadn't gone out of its way to confirm or deny. He knew that doubt would serve to undermine. Exactly his play.

He was enjoying and lapping up the limelight, receiving much domestic acclaim as the Russian people enjoyed this perverted span of control over the leading democracy in the world.

His people adored him, and that showed in the polls. Those who didn't, well, he would deal with them.

His army of bloggers, influencers, and hackers had evidently worked very well in further discrediting Clinton and promoting the Trump agenda.

He took satisfaction that the tactics first used by the CIA and the US government in the Arab Spring had the same destabilizing effect in the US.

By the time they were shut down, the damage had already been done, and the victory was his, and Russia's path was on the rise to power once more.

His meddling in elections elsewhere had gone largely unheeded, with the US story taking the lead and masking out the noise of antics elsewhere. The perfect cover. Just how the teachings of maskirovka had suggested.

He, like the rest of the world, had been watching Brexit and the potential further destabilization that represented. This created further opportunities for the motherland and her endeavors as the cracks started to show and gape wide open not just in the United Kingdom but across the European Union too.

He was also piling the pressure on former Soviet nations as the potential fragmentation of Europe impacted their own national security. Even Trump's threats to pull out of NATO played into his game plan perfectly.

He had instructed his military to make shows of strength around their airspace and sovereign waters, again sowing the seeds of doubt.

Under the radar, he had successfully taken back Crimea, and although a calculated risk, his unnamed, anonymous army completed the coup with relatively little fallout.

True, the sanctions were not ideal, but Russia had regained much of its strength, and they were nothing more than a pain in the side.

The prize of gaining back an all-year-round, all-weather port and access to the Black Sea for his navy was worth the sacrifices they had made.

He topped his china cup with Earl Grey, took a sip, and placed it back on the saucer, taking another bite of the madeleine. The snow had intensified outside, and the walkers, the romancers, and the children surely wanted to get back into the warmth and out of the Moscow elements.

He was pleased to be in his chair, by the window, looking out on his nation's capital.

First World Bank had been an experiment—an experiment that had worked very well indeed. In his strive to maximize cash flow and inbound foreign currency and profits, First World had been the perfect clearinghouse to turn dirty money clean. He was very happy with Dankov and his work. Since meeting him as a teenager, he always knew that he had potential.

After Sir Richard Steele's unfortunate suicide and the disappearance of Viktoria Saparov, then the suicide of her son, Nikita, he had sent in his own management team to settle down the ship and collect all the debt.

Under the guise of Brexit, he instructed to move the bank's headquarters to Athens. The Greeks were far more collaborative than the British ever were. They were open to Russian involvement, investments, and support, and that further drove doubt into the European Union project, heightening his chances to exploit and leverage the cracks— the EU being very unpopular, despite its bailouts, blamed for the austerity that had existed in the country for the past decade.

Russia's hunger for foreign investments was still keen, especially when it resulted in inbound cash flow during continued times of sanctions.

He had long been competing with China in befriending the African nations with long-term bumper loans for infrastructure projects, with almost payday loan levels of interest, terms, and returns. These were long bets.

Russian and Chinese firms were feverishly working away at creating the internet infrastructure and mobile networks that would enable the continent and allow them to harness the people and the revenues as a result, as they moved from the third to the second world and even beyond.

Many of these strategies had century-long timelines. Global strategies. These were his long-term plays and ones that he was certain would fuel Russia's return to its rightful place one day, probably far beyond his years on this earth.

Dankov's organization had been a pilot but one that also worked very well indeed. An old friend of the Kremlin, loyal to the motherland, Dankov had agreed to step across the line and create the state-backed underworld organization of the nation, building probably the most sophisticated dark army anywhere on the planet. It was well organized, well mobilized, intelligent, and highly trained, with plenty of political muscle and ways of getting things done that other such organizations didn't have the latitude to achieve.

Dankov was a power piece on his sixty-four-square game table.

It's one thing to have politicians on an organization's payroll, which of course happened all the time. It's a completely different thing when the government is funding your payroll—a very different and more potent style of partnership.

Genius. He smiled again.

Dankov's group had ventured into the world of drug distribution and the world of casinos—two great areas that recognized the value of cash, and a boatload of it, as king. Once the cash started flowing, the brainchild of the First World Bank came in. *Pure genius.*

The purchase of other assets grew the portfolio— convenience stores, discount supermarkets, even sports clubs like some English Premier League and Serie A—all cash-lucrative businesses. Cash was king in the venture. Just how he liked it.

This also gave way for him to do his less diplomatic work behind the scenes, as part of his strategy was to rebuild their reputation on the international stage.

Yes, the Crimea thing dinted that somewhat, but selling arms to countries and groups that weren't supposed to have them was less exposed—mercenaries for hire, whoever wanted them enough for the right price. Cash or equivalent liquid payment would do, with little or no tangible association back to the Kremlin.

Dankov's creation was perfect.

And as far as Dankov's latest venture in West Africa, grabbing an oil-rich nation, sliding into Africa, being the influential partner at the government level, and having the clearance to create a military outpost, these were all genius outcomes.

He didn't care for the Equatorial Guineans and their blatant greedy motives. He was fascinated by Bianca Blanca and her Mexico and LATAM smart moves. She was a talent to be watched. But what a creative partnership—again, testament to Dankov's organization.

He knew Dankov's father. They went to university together all those years ago in St. Petersburg. He always knew that Dankov had potential, and he had been proven right.

Then, all of that, covered with a generous layer of lies upon lies to make a great big maskirovka cake.

"Vkusnyye!" *Delicious! Perfect!*

Putin finished his tea, stood up, and looked at the now snowstorm outside his window. The square below was no longer visible, masked in white. He smiled once more at the thought of how the snow had wiped out the scene before him.

"Ideal, no?"

"Perfect."

PART IV

FUCK YOU

15
CUCKOO

March 2019
The Church of Saint Isabella's of Virgin Mary
Mexico City, Mexico
2:00 p.m.

BIANCA BLANCA SAT AT THE head of the conference table deep inside the Church of Isabella. The room was small yet elegant. The table itself was made from ancient and historical timber and topped with the finest black marble. She kept a neutral expression as she coolly looked from one man to the next, all fifteen of them. They were among the most powerful men and women in Mexico. Not bankers, lawmakers, politicians. Not government ministers, generals, or the church. They were dressed in their expensive suits, with designer sunglasses and a collection of some of the most beautiful watches available. Not over the top, not bling, not brash. Each of these people had style. They were proud, wealthy, and powerful because of the drug trade and their interests in it.

And they were vulnerable, just as Señor Mandito had been. *Yes,* she thought, *these men don't know how powerful I really am.*

She picked up the glass of ice water to her right and took a sip. For a quick moment, she allowed herself to luxuriate in her triumph and in the wisdom of her plan to influence great changes in the way the cartels conducted business. As she sat there, she delighted in the fact that she was arguably the most powerful woman in Mexico, Central America, and maybe South America.

She thought back to how the coming change began, to how she had originally been recruited by Viktoria Saparov as part of Dimitri Dankov's global expansion plans. She'd been planted as a sleeper in the Mexican cartel world, at least initially. Now, though, she'd cozied up to Putin and his pals almost as a partner in crime, as opposed to being a low-level agent. She'd come that far.

Originally from Cuba, Blanca's uncles led the Cuban Revolution. They were her heroes who replaced her dad, as he died in the struggles. It was in them that she believed. It was in them that she found the strength to survive those early years. They were her fathers in the absence of her own.

She moved to Mexico when she was twelve, regularly making trips back and forth to Havana and quickly getting noticed by one Señor Mandito. At age sixteen, she knew she was beautiful, and she put that to work. She had the dark eyes and the olive skin of her Cuban father and the blonde hair and tall, athletic frame of her mother, an American idealist from San Francisco. The fact that she spoke fluent English with no discernible accent was another important advantage in her climb to the top, that and the fact that she was as smart as a whip.

After Mandito took her under his wing, he hired a private teacher from England to help with his protégé and sent her to Oxford to study business and international politics. Upon her return, she began working her way up in the cartel under Mandito's careful guidance. As she got more responsibility, her ambitions soared to the point where she believed she should be the head of the organization, not Mandito, which was one reason why it had been easy for the Russians to recruit her.

As she surveyed the people in the room, she smiled slightly. Mandito hadn't counted on her taking over the whole show one day. And today was that day.

The diversification of the Mandito cartel was Blanca's brainchild. She had seen the writing on the walls long ago, and Viktoria Saparov's visit had sealed her point of view. Drugs were very dangerous—not only from the age-old *Tom & Jerry* antics with the DEA, FBI, and CIA but also the worsening gang rivalry that had expanded and killed tens of thousands over the years.

Since that time, she had driven their investments primarily into convenience retail and casinos. The other investments in real estate, hotels, and manufacturing were all big, good investments but not primarily cash businesses, and therefore, they didn't serve her purpose.

Mandito International now owned Yummy Stores, the largest convenience store chain in Mexico, with more than five thousand outlets on street corners across Mexico, a high percentage cash business, a place for the locals to pick up all their grocery needs—good for their distribution operations too.

The casino business was just an obvious one. When you want to get rid of or launder cash, then you go buy a casino or a casino owner. Blanca had decided on the former, although she had a couple of the latter on her payroll too. Casino owners had a habit of turning up when you didn't need them. All had bigger egos than their hands. All had more money than sense. All were unpredictable. In Blanca's opinion, it was better to own. Business results had proven her right.

News of the gas explosion at Casa Panorama had traveled very fast indeed, regardless of the fake news story, and that apparently Mandito wasn't even in residence. The fact was that Mandito was missing, and if the two-plus-two addition wasn't enough to work it out, then this meeting with Mandito's number two was, especially given the content of what she had to say.

Bianca Blanca addressed the audience. She was the only woman in the room.

"Gentlemen, it is with great sadness that I have called you together to announce the death of Señor Mandito. With Mandito's passing comes a new way." She looked around the table to see the poker faces and detect any element of shock among her audience.

"A way that he and I have been working on for many years. A new way. A new dawn for all of us around this table." The audience was listening attentively.

"A united Mexico, a stronger Mexico, a stronger cartel, *sobre todo*," she announced, looking around the table. It was obvious they needed more.

"Gentlemen, we are in a dangerous business, a very dangerous business, especially when we have cancer inside us. The cancer that we fight with each other. We kill our leaders, our soldiers, our people. My call is that it ends today. Ends for good."

Blanca knew these men were smart, but they'd been stuck in their old ways for so long. She understood why they might not be able to think of a new way. She would show them, and they'd go along, or they'd have to go.

She continued, "Before Señor Mandito died, he passed a resolution—a resolution to dissolve the Mandito cartel distribution operations and share them equally between the cartels in the room today. Equally. The total expense of the annual operation is $7 billion." She knew she had the element of surprise in the scale of their operations.

"And give or take a few million, that's half a billion dollars in operations for each of you."

She left the thought to tease them, but she also knew these were sharp people who had already done their own math the second she uttered the amount.

"So, for what in exchange?" She asked the audience the question they were asking themselves.

"As you know, Mandito International has legitimized its business operations, largely in the world of retail operations, in Mexico and beyond. This is a perfect way to help you turn dirty cash into clean. We will provide that service to all of you in exchange for this deal and this declaration between us and before you today."

She pointed at the center of the table where an odd-looking parchment paper, looking like it had been recovered from the Spanish Armada, sat ominously.

"This declaration of peace and cooperation between us here today is probably the most important document in Mexico's history since our country's recognition in 1821, three hundred years after our Spanish fathers arrived."

Although now dead, she knew that her mentor would be proud and that they were, in fact, doing this for the long-term good of their business, the nation, and the people of Mexico. He always had been a patriot and had seen the bigger prize. After all, all is fair in love, war, and business; she often reminded herself of Mandito's favorite saying.

She started to lay out the deal before her audience.

"One. We will dissolve the Mandito global distribution operations and distribute that equally among the fifteen of you.

"Two. You will channel cash proceeds through our Yummy Stores across the nation. You have over five thousand to choose from. We will set up a variety of payday-type loan accounts that exchange cash for checks.

"Three. For bigger, one-off transactions, you can use our network of casinos globally, and for even bigger transactions, our First World Bank investment vehicles.

"We know that this is a cash business. We get it, and we understand it." She held her hands up to her shoulders to demonstrate her point.

"In exchange, we ask you to put at least 80 percent of your business through Mandito International."

Most of the audience were writing notes in the pads provided on the meeting room table, along with the beautiful thousand-dollar Mont Blanc pens provided. The black pineapple design was Bianca's favorite, part of her curated experience and attention to detail in holding this meeting in the oldest church in Mexico City, Saint Isabella's of Virgin Mary, with a statue of her, dressed in blue, smiling and looking down upon them as they sat at the table, listening very carefully to every word now.

This was a serious business deal before them.

"We will take a management fee for all cash at a rate of 10 percent to cover administrative costs," she explained, smiling as though she was closing a transactional deal for a bank. She *was* closing a transactional deal for a bank, she thought. That made her smile at her audience more.

Bianca did notice that one member of the audience was not taking notes, Paulo Mancini: dark, swept-back hair with hints of gray; dark brown eyes, almost black; dressed in an immaculate beige, lightweight Hugo Boss suit, pink Thomas Pink dress shirt, brown Dunhill shoes, and no socks. He was leaning back in his chair, Patek Philippe watch on his wrist, staring at Bianca, listening to each and every word, serious poker face but smiling eyes. Smiling eyes at Bianca.

She smiled back at Mancini. Blanca had not finished her pitch. She was enjoying herself.

There were some intakes of breath from her last part of the deal. She may have to persuade them on the 10 percent.

"This cartel charter maps out very clear territories for each of us. We will meet once every quarter, in peace. We will work with each other to protect our business against our common enemies. We will garner support from those who have influence, together. We will move forward *together, in peace.*"

She caught Mancini's eye and his thought. She looked at him directly. Purposeful, serious, and ruthless if necessary. Powerful.

"Some of you may hear this and think of some speech for the nation, but let me tell you here and now, this charter before you could become the most important in our nation's history, and you here today are the pioneers of our future.

"Safety in numbers, legitimate recycling. No more killings. Peace and profitability.

"Questions?"

Despite the thick walls of the church, Bianca could still hear the faint thud and flutter of the helicopters above, flying air cover for security purposes. The various cartels brought their own security details, and each contingent was wary of the other. She knew that a miscalculation could turn the meeting into a bloodbath. Still, she sensed that the men in the room knew how momentous this deal could be, if everyone cooperated.

The Union Club
Greek Street, London, United Kingdom
3:00 p.m.

As they wrapped up their briefing, James flicked to the BBC News to check the latest on Brexit and what Trump had been up to that day, both habits nowadays—a daily ritual for many, which was indenting soap opera ratings in the UK and around the world.

Bella and the rest of the group listened to the latest status reports about blundered deadlines, clandestine political groups taking position, and the seemingly resolute European leaders standing firm.

She heard the latest on the Mueller investigation saga, the indictments, and the latest schoolyard bully attempts by Trump to get his wall. Crooked lawyers, alleged secret meetings, allegations of various secret liaisons, including glamour models and porn stars, and Twitter rants.

"People have become almost immune to this claptrap nonsense," stated Beecham as the others nodded and agreed.

The BBC News channel flipped to a breaking news story.

It grabbed the room's attention in the melodramatic fashion that it was designed to do.

"In a shocking announcement today, GroMart, the global retailing giant and supermarket chain, was involved in a takeover that would net the shareholders $300 billion in an unprecedented deal. With GroMart operations across the US and notably MARKA in the UK, this deal, if nothing else, is an indication that at least some investors still believe in the brick-and-mortar retail model, widely seen as being under threat globally. The new owners, Mandito International, in a deal funded by the First World Bank, made a statement."

The room went immediately silent. Deadly silent.

"GroMart CEO Ken Johnson said, 'This is a strategic play, and we believe that with our new partners, Mandito International, GroMart can become stronger than ever and transcend our consumer-centered offering in places around the world, that with greater local infrastructure and support, we can grow our global share of the grocery market, including in Mexico and across South America, Africa, and Russia.'"

"Blah. Blah fucking blah, blah," Bob said.

Bella noticed Mitch twizzling his ring, not for the first time that day. It wasn't a good sign.

The announcement finished as quickly as it started, concluding that this was a mega deal brokered by the First World Bank. It made some mention of the apparent suicides of its chairman, Sir Richard Steele, and its investment guru, one Nikita Saparov, in 2016 and closed.

"If that isn't enough confirmation of our analysis, then nothing else is," Beecham said. "This isn't just a series of unrelated incidents. This is a culmination of a much longer-term strategy than we had ever realized, and it's all coming together before our very eyes."

Bella's mind raced. The global implications of the scheme floored her. Her team would have to disrupt those plans, no matter the cost, no matter the dangers from the Russians or the cartels.

"So, what's our next move?" Mac asked.

16
CHELSEA DAGGER

Chelsea High Street
London, United Kingdom
3:45 p.m.

BELLA HAD NOTICED THAT MITCH was unusually quiet during the briefing, maybe for obvious reasons. He had lived a life full of danger and lived to tell the tales, but now he knew that Dankov was still alive and apparently plotting revenge and payback. It was enough to unsettle anyone, including Mitch. The fact that Yee, the Dog, had been taken out disconcerted her. If Dankov could get to him, then he could get to her and her dad.

The incident back in DC had spooked her. What she thought was her bit of fun was actually much more sinister. The fact that they hired three thugs to do their work was a departure from their modus operandi and indication to her that they were seeking to inflict pain and harm, not go the full measure and take her out. If they had wanted the latter outcome, the quality of her suitors would have been very different, although she was confident that the outcome would have been similar. She would have swapped the wrench for her Glock, a more terminal situation for her enemies.

As the team dispersed, Bella watched as Mac went over to Mitch and gave him a bear hug and a pat on the back, whispering in his ear. She was close enough to hear. "Dankov and whose fucking army?" he said with a smile. Mitch looked at the floor and agreed, unconvincingly. "What the fuck's up, mate?" Mac asked.

"We've got this." Bella intervened, sensing one of Mitch's silent moments and rescuing him from the conversation.

She knew Mitch like no other, despite friends and colleagues like Mac who had been around Mitch in tight spots for years. Bella was connected at a different level and could see through his emotions.

When he moved to the veterans' shelter in the Presidio, back in San Francisco, no one really understood, especially her mum, Angela, but Bella did. She had witnessed his gradual withdrawal over the years. With each of his mysterious trips, and upon each return, it got more intense. There was more sadness deep in his eyes.

Ever since she was kidnapped by Dankov's people all those years ago, Mitch began to withdraw, his distance being a safety net for his loved ones. Although they'd never discussed it, she concluded that he'd separated from Angela in part to protect her, in case bad guys like Dankov's thugs came after her, and in part because he had trouble living with the posttraumatic stress disorder she knew he had. He didn't want to inflict his pain on her or her mum. Bella looked at her father and gave him a reassuring smile and a hug and a quick kiss on the cheek.

They all said goodbye to check out of their various separate lodgings and check into the comfort and safety of Beecham's London townhouse.

Bella and Mitch left together. They turned right down Greek Street and into Soho until they disappeared into the crowds, both Bella and Mitch checking that they weren't being followed. They slowed down their pace to engage in conversation.

"Dad, are you okay?"

"How's Langley?" he asked.

"Don't change the subject. I asked you what's wrong. You've seemed out of it all day long."

"Nothing's wrong," Mitch said, his voice glum.

"Don't lie to me. I know you too well for that."

Mitch stopped walking and placed his hands on her shoulders, giving them a gentle squeeze. "Look, I don't want to talk about it, okay? Can you just drop it?"

Bella sighed as he let go of her shoulders. "Have it your way, Dad. It's just that I'm worried about you. But okay. I'll drop it. For now."

"So, how's work going?" he asked again.

"It's okay. Full of fun."

"Yep, I heard."

She looked at him quizzically.

"The three thugs you took out the other night."

She looked at him again, this time with a grimace of anger.

"Fifth time in the last few months," he noted.

"What is this, Dad? A fucking inquisition?"

"No, just a dad keeping an eye out for his daughter."

"What do you mean—you or Chip?"

"Both."

"Anyway, I'm not talking about me. I'm asking about you. Then you flipped it over to focus on me. Cute, Dad. Real cute."

They walked in silence for a few blocks until Mitch broke it.

"It's nice that you worry about me, Bella," he said. "That makes me feel loved, and that's a big help right now. Believe me. It really is."

"I love you, Dad. You know that. And I know you're probably struggling with PTSD, even if you won't admit it to me or anyone else."

Mitch exhaled loudly. "Yeah, I got it. Who wouldn't after what I've seen and done?"

Bella could only imagine. Mitch never talked about what he did, but she knew things could get hairy in the field in the blink of an eye. "I'm sorry," she said. She reached out and took his hand.

"Churchill used to call it his black dog. I guess I have a whole kennel, and this shit with Dankov doesn't help matters."

"Yeah, tell me about it."

"I'll slog on through this, Peanut. Don't worry. Or at least try not to worry. But we both need to be careful, Bella, on the lookout. I spoke with Chip. He told me about the stash of cash in the backpack, the photos, and the connection to Dankov's casino." Bella felt his glare as he searched for more.

"Well, if they were serious, they wouldn't have sent those three idiots," she said.

Mitch nodded slowly. "Yes, that's right. But sending guys like that to scare you shows they wanted to inflict pain."

Bella had considered this before. She didn't want to think about what they had in mind for her. She felt disgusted and violated just thinking about it now. "Well, I was the one who inflicted the pain," she said.

"You sure as hell did!" he said with a laugh. "You kicked some real ass."

Bella laughed along with him and then got serious again. "I'm amazed that Dankov survived the bomb," she said.

"Me too. It's like these Russians are like fuckin' cats. They got nine lives."

"Like you say. We'll muddle through. You'll muddle through, Dad. I know you will. You'll chase those demons away, just like always."

Mitch stopped, raised both arms straight up, and said, "Demons be gone!"

Some passersby gave him strange looks.

"You're nuts, you know that?" she said. "Come on. Put your arms down. People are staring!"

That old familiar twinkle was in his eyes at that moment. His playfulness, his abiding love for her and for her mum, it was all reflected in a split second. Then it was gone again. They continued walking to their hotel.

"How's Mum?" he asked.

She knew that Mitch had barely been home in the last twelve months, taking trips at will to Santiago and Shanghai, a couple of trips to London, one to Sydney, a tour of Australia, with Hong Kong and Kuala Lumpur on the way back, stopping in Oslo and Copenhagen, then to Canada before heading home. And then he moved into the Presidio in an informal separation from her mum. She'd persuaded him to move back home, and he did, at least temporarily. For now. He was running away from himself, and she knew it. It started with his work at the Presidio. He'd become a volunteer, board director, and governor. Combine that with his trips, and he was basically never around.

"She's fine," Bella said. "Same old, same old, I'm afraid." Glancing over at him, she said, "She misses you. I miss you."

"I know, I know," he said. "Okay, you said you'd drop it, so let's drop it for now. Okay, Peanut?"

"Deal."

They passed a jeweler, Avanti, and they both recognized the name and logo from the past. "Hey, isn't this the same place that you bought that pink diamond ring for Mum?"

He looked up and nodded. "Sure is." She recalled, after his trip to London years ago, him returning home with the stunning pink diamond ring he bought for Angela. They had both seen it in some swanky magazine as they were holidaying in Thailand, and months later, on a trip to London, he had traipsed around Sloane Square for hours, trying to find the shop.

"I think she wore it all of ten times," he joked with a hint of annoyance.

"She cherished it. It was special, just for special occasions," Bella said, defending her mum.

"Come on. Let's go get a drink," he said as they came across the Fox & Hounds on Passmore Street.

Mitch opened the door for Bella and gestured for her to go in. They took a pair of stools at the bar and ordered two shots of Balblair whisky and two pints of Guinness. They clinked glasses, said, "Cheers," took a wee nip, and slurped a big sip of the Dublin Gold.

Without the previous tension or the line of inquiry, they were both relaxed. Just two people, father and daughter, on their own, together, enjoying their own company. It had been a while.

They talked about Brexit and Trump. They talked about Angela, home, and Langley. Mitch kept ribbing her about her new nickname, Rambo. She kicked him and told him to fuck off in a jovial, loving way. They were more than father and daughter. Mitch and Bella were best friends; they always had been. They talked about Blackie's Pasture back home in Tiburon, their preferred regular stroll by the water, and the statue of the old horse himself. They talked about Argus, Uncle Paul, and Badger Bell, leaving Nikita and Jimmy out of the conversation. They talked about a fun past and hopefully more fun for the future.

Bella knew to stay away from the many darker subjects that they both knew would wind them up. Bella had healthy respect to let these things be. Mitch ordered another round as they continued to shoot the breeze.

The old black, wooden door of the Fox & Hounds opened, and in walked two men—tall, wide shouldered, with tattoos, but not those of the Barmy Army, another army that both Mitch and Bella were all too familiar with. Bella had spotted them earlier as they approached Greek Street, later near the jeweler, and now again in the Fox & Hounds. It was Ivan and Ivan from Beecham's briefing. Bella's senses went on immediate high alert. She nudged Mitch and nodded in the direction of the two Russians.

"Yeah," he said, "I see 'em. Not too subtle, are they?"

"About as subtle as a lion in a chicken coop."

Mitch cocked an eyebrow. "How's that again?"

Bella laughed. "Just made that one up. You like it?"

"Not really. I think you could come up with something better."

"I'll try. Next time."

Bella noted their position relative to that of the watchers. She and Mitch were seated to the right side of the horseshoe bar, tucked away behind the pillar that obscured them from immediate and obvious view but where they could observe the new visitors to the bar. This was always their modus operandi, something that Mitch had taught her as a child: always be aware of your surroundings—diligent and prepared for anything.

Immediately, Bella felt the hair on the back of her neck stand on end.

The two men sat down on opposite sides of the pillar, no line of sight to Mitch and Bella. They were just two people on the other side of the four-by-four redbrick column. They ordered vodka of course. It was no coincidence they were in the proximity, but maybe they had slipped up, let their guard down, and stumbled across the Fox & Hounds coincidently. Maybe, but Bella didn't believe in coincidences.

Apart from play fighting when Bella was a kid and role-playing different scenarios, this was the first time they had been in high danger together. Bella was excited. She didn't want a fight, but she knew she and her father would finish one if it happened. She glanced over at Mitch, noted that he was excited too. He was twizzling his ring again, a sure sign that he was ready.

The two Russian bruisers were both moaning about the terrible vodka, the London streets, and that they couldn't find what they were looking for. Bella knew enough Russian to know that. Maybe this meeting was coincidental.

"Fucking wankers," Mitch said at almost a shout.

The Fox & Hounds was very quiet, ready for its evening influx of Sloaners in this swanky, expensive, and international area, even for London. This old traditional London boozer had kept all its quaintness and originality, but its clientele had been truly transformed into a new hip crowd. They hadn't arrived yet. By the looks of the bar staff, a remnant from the old boozer days, they probably hadn't seen a bar fight for years and probably missed it if the truth be known.

One of the bruisers tried to catch a glimpse of them around the corner, and Mitch turned his back to obscure the view. The biggest of the two, about six feet five, scar down the side of his chin, bald, and with a gold tooth, scraped his stool back on the slate slabs, stood up, and made his way around the corner to where the pool table still survived the foie gras, escargot, and Chablis.

He towered above Mitch, who sat motionless on his stool.

"Chto ty skazal, blyad?" (What did you say, you fucker?)

"How the fuck is our friend Dankov today? How many laps did he run around the palace this morning?"

The big man just stared down at Mitch, fists clenched.

"Don't you have any poison pills for me? Umbrellas with Polonium-210 on the tip, any bad fashion advice, any fucking bedtime stories?"

"You are in big trouble, my friend," said the big Russian, at which point his shooting partner came around the corner.

"Well, fuck me. It's Ivan the fucking Terrible and Ivan the Terribler!" Mitch mocked, still sitting on his stool.

"How is Dmitri fucking Dankov, boys?" he taunted.

"Did he send you over here?" Bella asked, noting that people were hurrying out of the bar, anticipating a fight or possibly something even worse.

"What do you think, sweetie?" the big thug said.

"Did Dankov brief you?" Mitch asked, his voice calm, cool, and collected. "Did he brief you on who the fuck I am? Of course not. Too bad for you."

None of them broke eye contact. Now the bar was completely empty, except for the combatants. Bella felt her heartrate increase. Sweat formed along her hairline. Out of the corner of her eye, she saw the front door of the bar open. To her utter relief, in walked Mac, who had obviously gotten the text she'd sent after she saw the Russians enter the bar.

"Now, what do we have here?" he asked.

"Some of Dankov's boys," Bella said.

"Well, you don't say!" Mac said as he slowly approached the bar. "Isn't that interesting."

The biggest guy leaned forward and got in Mitch's face. "He sent us to kill you and your shit little girl. And that's exactly what we're gonna do."

Mitch responded calmly, "Well, Ivan and Ivan." He nodded to number two. "That may be more difficult than you had actually bargained for because the three of us are about to give you a good lesson on why that really isn't a good idea."

Enraged, Bella leaped from the barstool, spun around to build momentum, and body kicked Ivan No. 1 right in the balls, causing him to hunch over. She whacked him with a serious uppercut as Mac speared him through the right eye with a broken pool cue, killing him instantly. It happened so quickly that all Ivan No. 2 could do was watch the milliseconds of violence before him. Mitch turned to him.

"What do you want to do, Ivan? Should I send you back to Dankov to give him the warning that I am not going to just roll over? I don't fucking think so. What good would that do? I think my best option is to put you down here and now and send the message to others like you that you don't fucking mess with me."

"What do you think of that, Ivan?" Mac asked, getting up into the thug's face. He stepped back, keeping his arms and fists on guard, ready for an attack.

"Oh, fuck this," Mitch said. He pulled his Browning Hi-Impact 9 mm, pointed at Ivan's forehead, and fired. The big Russian dropped like a sack of potatoes.

"Well, look at the mess you made," Mac said, nodding toward the dead Russian, who was missing most of the back of his skull. Blood and gray brain matter covered the floor around the corpse.

"Couldn't be helped," Mitch said. "If you wanna make an omelet, you gotta break some eggs."

"Uh-huh. Yeah, right. Well, I guess we've got breakfast for three all right."

"I think we'd better get the hell out of here," Bella said.

And they did, leaving the bodies for the local police to worry about. Bella led the way out the front door.

"This way," Mac said, turning to his right. "I'm parked about two blocks away."

A few minutes later, they arrived at Mac's Range Rover. As Bella opened the front passenger side door, she looked over and smiled at Mac. "Thanks, Mac." Mac smiled back at her and winked.

Mitch said, "Pretty impressive, Ella Bella Super Duper Hula Hoopa." They all laughed as their posttraumatic tension released. Bella had learned over the years that humor was a good way to do that.

Mac piped in, ribbing his old friend, "Did yer not have yer spectacles with yer today, Mitch?" referencing the point-blank nature of his coup de grace. They all got the reference and laughed together.

17
GOOD WORK

Barkli Apartments
Ostozhenka, Moscow, Russian Federation
7:00 a.m.

DMITRI DANKOV GOT TO THE top of the stairs outside the plush Barkli apartments located just three miles from the Kremlin, within easy reach of his superiors, his security protection, and access to information whenever he needed it.

Stretching down from his morning ritual, a five-mile, fast-paced walk, his rehabilitation was complete, and now he just had to keep in shape to make the most of his circumstances. A big man, muscular yet athletic, he had been through many things in his life, and he would get through this and move on.

One of the less athletic, iron-pumping bodyguards passed him a face towel as he wiped down the mild perspiration from his face. The burns on his right side, although now healed, still stung as a reminder of what happened.

He walked down the steps at the outside of the apartment building, giving the first sign of a limp as he traversed downward and then arrived at the front door. An entranceway with a long, dark corridor and a white marble floor gave the impression of a secret entrance to a secret compartment. This opened up to the black-and-gold reception area, where a manned security desk kept inquisitive intruders from entering the building. It was a place filled with prestigious people, all wealthy, many connected, and many forming the hierarchy of Russia's most coveted and secret personnel.

Dmitri Dankov belonged to all those categories.

He entered the gold elevator and made his way to the top floor and his penthouse suite. His security detail swept the apartment before Dankov dismissed them for his own privacy. The heavily armored, gold-plated door was bolted with four independent locks that used fingerprint recognition as a means to open.

Despite his past and the incident in Moscow, he wasn't a nervous man; in fact, quite the opposite. It wasn't that he was careless, because he was a very deliberate, purposeful man who did everything that he did for a reason. His lack of nervousness was more self-confidence and, beyond that, a level of self-assured arrogance that he belonged to something bigger, his group of senior Russian comrades, patriots of the motherland, a hero of the empire.

Alongside one another, arm in arm, they would together get Russia back in its rightful place as the king of Europe and a global superstate and leader on the world stage.

For too long, Russia had been regarded as the sulky but surly boy in the playground that no one really talked to, as they were frightened of what reaction they would get from engaging. Russia in years gone by had also played to that caricature and fueled the level of uncertainty and distrust. The Russian Empire had matured from that churlish behavior and was working hard in creating a more approachable, collaborative persona with the world, but its old enemies remained skeptical, as they probably should.

Dankov grabbed an orange juice from the fridge and his tablet and walked over to his balcony overlooking the rooftops of the Ostozhenka district below him. The morning sunshine glinted off the Kremlin a little distance away, its ornate towers and domes—a constant reminder of what he stood for, what he was building, what he and Russia were rebuilding. Dankov was at the very heart of this new Russian Empire.

Dankov was clearly recognized as the architect of Temnaya Armiya, the Dark Army, originally created in times of sovereign weakness, to develop ways to attract much-needed foreign currencies.

It had quickly become a lucrative source of international funding for domestic efforts and their phoenixlike cause.

Thanks to Dankov and his initiatives, he had fast-tracked the recovery efforts and opened up an arm that could carry out some of the finer and darker arts on the world stage—that, with the help of maskirovka and the Kremlin's public relations machine, could be quickly buried and forgotten, the truth hidden from the world's public eye with lie upon lie upon lie.

In fact, the Russian people, the patriots, took pleasure in seeing how some of his exploits had worked out, deciphering the press to what was underneath. The government press had even coined a phrase to mock the rest of the world: *Of course Russia was to blame* for the Patriots winning the Super Bowl, Taylor Swift making number one, the Mueller investigation, the indictment of presidential lawyers and confidantes, the rigging of the US election. The irony was that they had managed to turn the tale to the point of national humor, reacting to and resisting the notion that the surly schoolboy was up to his old tricks.

He had set the organization up like a corporation, with him as CEO and with chief operating officers in the Americas, APAC, Asia Pacific and EMEA, Europe, the Middle East, and Africa. Each COO was tasked with securing partners in the regions to establish mutual business interests across a whole range of often illicit activities, including drug distribution, arms, gambling, and people trafficking—all with the notion of generating big cash profits.

These illicit activities had a destabilizing effect on some of their enemies of the state. As Dankov made profits, their people got more hooked on the drugs they distributed. The guns they exported fueled crime and social unrest. Even their sex trafficking cut into the moral grounding of these so-called great nations.

Beyond the cash generation, his Dark Army had also been the cover for some darker work on behalf of the motherland. His associates had also supported various campaigns to destabilize local, regional, and national politics.

Social media, invented by the Americans and used as a weapon for the first time in the Arab Spring to undermine governments, was one of the vehicles in which he had invested to sway voters' opinions, most notably in the Brexit vote, designed to destabilize the notion of the European Union and all that represented in the dilution of the Russian Empire and coalition. Then, of course, the US election.

The organization, assembly, fueling, and powering of rebel forces inside of Crimea was another great victory for Dankov and his Dark Army.

The organization had been hit by the events of Operation Argus, or so it was named, with the loss of two of its COOs and the damned near loss of the CEO too.

Dankov was still alive to tell the tale, and he was back with a vengeance.

The tentacles that his organization had created ran deep and were intertwined.

He answered his secure satellite phone.

"Utro." Dankov listened to the familiar voice at the end of the line.

"Korosho." (Good, good.)

"Did they all sign up to the agreement?"

"Otlichno." (Very good.)

"And the terms?"

"Fantastika." (Excellent.)

"Good work, my friend. Very good work."

The voice on the phone went on to explain the shooting of two associates in a London bar. Word had it that Mitch and his crew were involved. Dankov asked to be kept informed and hung up.

He looked inside the apartment and saw Oxsana rising from the bedroom. He watched her as she poured a glass of orange juice, her dark, ruffled hair not detracting from her natural beauty—dark, exotic eyes and pouting lips, with pajamas silhouetting her long legs and voluptuous curves.

He left the cold December Moscow air, slid the doors behind him, closed the blinds, and went to warm himself.

The Church of Saint Isabella's of Virgin Mary
Mexico City, Mexico
6:00 p.m.

Paulo Mancini was the last of the cartel lords remaining. He was one of the affiliates but an important and powerful one—head of Los Rastrojos, controlling Colombia and therefore a critical partner.

Unlike some of the others who had grown up on the hard streets of Mexico, like Blanca, he had a relative silver-spoon upbringing under the wings of a willing and generous sponsor.

Mancini, a gamekeeper-cum-poacher had formally been the commander of the anticartel forces, until an attack on his patrol. He had witnessed how the Colombian government had colluded with the cartels and set up an ambush that killed twenty-two of his own men and friends.

After that, he changed sides, and instead of ruling and raping his country, he decided he would buck the trend in leading and nurturing his country and his people. In his province, he was respected, not feared. He was admired. He was their leader, and they were his people. Paulo Mancini, like Bianca Blanca, was a different breed. They were the new, smarter leaders who, beyond politicians, had a greater opportunity to achieve great things.

He turned to Blanca and let out a slow round of applause but with genuine admiration and appreciation for what she had just pulled off.

Of course, this wasn't the first time they had seen the charter; she had taken great pains to socialize, share, and reach an agreement before this seminal meeting.

She had pulled it off. They had asked their questions, satisfied their levels of distrust, and negotiated the deal from 10 percent to 8. Both Blanca and the cartel leaders were happy with that, and, God willing, she had just fixed the cartels of Mexico and Central America to a much better solution and outcome for all. Bianca Blanca had just unified the cartels, potentially brought peace, and set up Mandito International as a major, legitimate force to be reckoned with.

"Pure genius." Mancini smiled at Blanca. "You, my *señorita,* are one class act! Now let's go for a drink and celebrate."

They kissed, and off they went into their shared black, armor-plated SUV for a celebratory, private, and very secure dinner.

Hilton Malabo
Equatorial Guinea, West Africa
10:00 p.m.

Josh Penbury sat in the hotel bar at the Hilton Malabo, another crisis zone, another hotel bar, another crew around him,

"Why the fuck do I do this, Mark? Tell me, why the fuck do we do this shit-ass job? Can you fucking tell me?" He leaned across the table past the half-empty bottle of Johnny

Walker to pass another Marlboro Light and get a light from his friend's lighter.

"We've been in this game too long, my friend. This isn't very fucking funny anymore. Another country, another fucking point to prove, another fucking war zone. What ever happened with graduating from school and becoming a Wall Street columnist or a fucking *Hello* magazine reporter? Why the fuck did we end up with this gig, in the shittiest, most inhospitable shitholes of the world? Eh? Eh, Mark?"

Mark Ogilvy sat across the table from Josh and smiled. "You silly fucker, Josh. You know we fucking love this gig. It's the whisky talking. Tomorrow you'll be right as rain and up on your game, just like you always are. You are a true-blue professional. You love it really." Mark smiled and winked at his colleague, having consumed far less of the Johnny Walker than his friend.

"Come on, let's head out and go to the Bello Norte."

"Are you fucking serious? With all that's going on in this city? You want to head to a fucking strip club while there is anarchy outside?"

"Fuck it. Why not? Have you lost your sense of adventure?"

Josh grinned at his friend, knowing that it wouldn't take much convincing for him to go along with the plan. He'd been fond of Mark since they first met at the University of California at Berkeley, where they both studied journalism. They stuck together after graduation when they both joined the CRN News Network.

A cockroach, big, fat, the size of a small mouse, ventured up on the tabletop and started making its way across. Josh, with a rolled-up copy of the *New York Times*, slammed it with full power, and the contents of the wee beasty, eggs and all, and its putrid, sweet smell filled the air between them.

"I fucking hate this shithole," Josh said.

He was tired, bone tired. The current assignment was an extension of a series of grueling gigs. They had both covered Iraq, Afghanistan, then Venezuela, and now, to put the icing on the cake, "Equatorial fucking Guinea."

Out of all four, Equatorial Guinea was by far on the very bottom of that mediocre list.

"Come on, man. Let's head to Ekzotika for a laugh."

"You mean the fucking Russian whore house?"

"Fuck it! Why not?"

"Come on, you drunken, fucking bum. Why not? Let's go, potential fucking war zone or not."

"You stupid fucker," Mark said. "Come on. Let's go."

They left the bar and headed to Ekzotika, an enclave of debauchery for the rich and wealthy of Malabo and the many visiting contractors to this oil-rich land of West Africa. Unlike the others, this was Russian-owned, and therefore the menu was more varied and international as compared with the other West Africa shit pits. If there was a star rating for these types of places, then this would be a three star establishment in the sea of one-star establishments surrounding it.

Josh stumbled in with Mark at his side. He took a table, ordered a bottle of bourbon, and sat down. The girls followed the money and joined them. A couple of quick nods and a couple of lines of coke later, Josh was now calmer and settled into the debauchery of the evening. He had a few hours of fun to drown out this shithole. Then he would be ready for their next day's reporting.

TAB: That's Africa, baby!

The Malabo Government Building
Equatorial Guinea, East Africa
10:00 a.m.

The next morning, Josh awoke with a headache and could hear the chanting in the distance. He turned over to look at his watch. "Fuck. It's ten in the fucking morning. What the fuck?" He spent a moment orientating himself, lying on his back in his bed, the ceiling fan whirring above him, considering the debauchorous events of the previous evening. He reached for a bottle of water by his bedside and took a big swig. "I fucking hate this shithole." He reminded himself of his current plight.

The crowd had been gathering and multiplying since seven that morning outside the Malabo Government Building, residence to the president of Equatorial Guinea. Built in 1965, the four-story sandstone building, protected by its iron gates, with a typical lack of class, looked like a cross between Buckingham Palace and a Home Depot store.

Since the coup d'état in 1979 when the sitting president assassinated his own uncle to take power, this grubby little oil nation on the west coast of Africa had seen little political opposition to his rule, mainly because opposition wasn't authorized. In the 2002 presidential elections, the ruling party won in a landslide victory with 97.1 percent of the vote.

In recent months, on the run-up to the upcoming elections, the level of volume had risen substantially, with the official minority but underlying popular vote being led by Celestino Romada Racale, a young, Oxford-educated academic turned activist who, seemingly like many others, was sick of the corruption of the nation and its leaders and the apparent syphoning off of the country's wealth just to line the pockets of the already wealthy, in total disregard of the poor.

This was a country where the gross domestic product per capita was $32,000 a year. Yet the majority of the country survived on less than a dollar a day. The imbalance of wealth and disregard of its people was the main cornerstone of the opposition.

Worse for wear, the two reporters headed downtown to see what all the fuss was about to maybe capture a story for their network. At the end of the day, that was why they were here, Mark reminded Josh sarcastically.

It wasn't quite clear how the resurgence of the rebellion had started and how it was catching the interest of global media, given all that was happening in the world. Was this all fueled by outside forces in the first place? That was the question.

Either way, the crowd outside of the government building had swelled to almost two thousand, with their banners and their signs and their chants to bring down the current regime.

"Racale in, Mbasogo out!"

"Government out, Racale in!"

"Democracy in, dictatorship out!"

"Racale in, people win!"

The crowd chanted as they marched to the big iron gates.

Racale was the front-runner, the only runner, and was gaining a lot of international support for his candidacy and legitimization to replace the current and corrupt regime.

Dotted in the crowd were men with black hoodies, clearly not countrymen, organized, briefed, armed with batons, coordinating the chants like football hooligans, stirring up the crowd.

Half a dozen armored vehicles rolled down the plaza behind the crowd, loudspeakers bellowing out to the crowd to disperse. The chanting got louder, and the vehicles got nearer. The water cannons turned on, and the chanting became angrier.

"Racale in, Mbasogo out!"

"Government out, Racale in!"

"Democracy in, dictatorship out!"

"Racale in, people win!"

"Leave now and go back home," came across the speaker of the armored vehicles, water cannons spewing water over the crowd, knocking protestors off their feet as the sheer power of the jets hit them.

Ignoring the calls for order, the crowd grew louder and angrier and continued their chant for freedom.

"Racale in, Mbasogo out!"

"Government out, Racale in!"

"Democracy in, dictatorship out!"

"Racale in, people win!"

A wave of foot soldiers and police threw smoke grenades and tear gas cannisters into the crowd, disorienting and temporally blinding. The chanting dimmed somewhat, but their anger grew.

Skirmishes started with the protestors and the armed soldiers, batons thrashing, boots kicking, protestors fighting back with their own weapons and those of the black hoodies, batons, sticks, and clubs.

As the tear gas faded and the effects subsided, the chanting started again, with one of the armored vehicles being turned over on its back by a group of one hundred or so protestors.

"Racale in, Mbasogo out!"

"Government out, Racale in!"

"Democracy in, dictatorship out!"

"Racale in, people win!"

A big cheer came from the crowd as the armored vehicle flipped and wobbled like a tortoise rolling on its back. One of the black hoodies tossed their own smoke grenade inside another of the armored vehicles, with its occupants quickly making an exit and getting attacked by the protestors.

The commander of the government forces ordered the plastic bullets for crowd control, and as the soldiers fired them, they bounced off the tarmac, bouncing up, breaking bones, smashing skulls.

More water cannons, more tear gas, and the combination of the plastic bullets was enough to quell and disperse the crowd and silence the chants. The police rounded up those protestors who hadn't escaped, destined for incarceration in some secret place—punishments, beatings, and potentially never seeing freedom again.

Josh and Mark stuck with it through the day, despite their hangovers, and managed to record a series of respectable reports that would be winging their way back to the network for distribution and consumption worldwide.

"You know nobody's interested in this shit, right?" offered Penbury.

"What do you mean? Of course they are. What the fuck is wrong with you recently?"

"They're all in the fucking middle-class homes, with their middle-class mortgages and their middle-class cars, jobs, and lives. They don't care about what's going on down here. They've had enough of news and are only interested in what's going on in their own fucking bubbles."

"That's a bit harsh, isn't it?" countered Ogilvy.

Josh was just tired of it all—the lifestyle, the hypocrisy, the turmoil in the world. He desperately needed a break, and he figured Mark did too.

"They're sick of hearing all this crap. They've even stopped listening to Trump and his fucking manic tweets in the middle of the night. They've become immune, deaf to the noise. Prefer to watch *Modern fucking Family* or *Family fucking Feuds* than watch this shit that doesn't affect them on the other side of the world."

"I think you need a vacation, my friend," Mark said.

"This is maskirovka at its best, you know?"

"What the fuck are you talking about now?" Mark asked.

"This is it. Fill the press with so much crap that the audience no longer knows what's important or not. They don't know what the truth is anymore. They give up caring, get bored, leaving these fuckers to do what they want even in the full glare of the world. They are more interested in the next fixer-upper or fucking Love Island."

"Like I say, you need a vacation, maybe a very long vacation, Josh. Have you ever thought about getting into something else that you actually enjoy? Like being a fucking tiddlywinks commentator on one of the sports channels?

Penbury threw his pencil at Ogilvy and laughed.

"Fuck off. Let's go back to the hotel and grab a beer."

18
FIRST WORLD

First World Bank
Canary Wharf, London, United Kingdom
8:00 a.m.

SHERI BRODIE WALKED INTO THE glass-fronted lobby of First World Bank, Canary Wharf, on the banks of the River Thames.

Sheri was a career woman, a corporate woman, a go-getter, and now the CEO of the First World Bank. Although the actual registered headquarters of the bank had moved to Athens, for all intents and purposes, nothing had changed; this was still the public headquarters of probably the most successful bank in recent times.

Dressed in her designer blue, slim-fit suit, hugging her tall and very womanly curves, her Jimmy Choo's, Gucci handbag, Piaget watch, plain pearl necklace, and Burberry blue overcoat, Sheri was a sharp dresser and looked the part of the first female chief executive officer of any London-based bank.

The security guards all but stood at attention as she breezed in with her carefully coiffured blonde bob and her corporate but friendly smile. She strode past reception and said good morning to the receptionists in her Texan drawl.

Her rise to the top hadn't been easy. After the sad suicide of Sir Richard Steele, former president and CEO, then the tragic loss of Nikita Saparov, their mercurial predictor of sorts, and then the takeover by the Trakkai Investment Group, she was the last person standing to take over the reins, which she did gladly. It was her corporate dream come true. She had made it.

She stepped into the elevator and headed to the executive floor, the executive suite, and her office.

Things had settled down. Although in days gone by, the cut and the thrust of daily operations had been exciting, Sheri was enjoying her figurehead role now, meeting and greeting, making investor calls, doing investment road shows, signing big checks, and receiving big checks. Today was a big check day.

They had received two, $500 million deposits to place in a jointly funded operating account. The parties were anonymous and wanted to remain that way, and she had clearance from Moscow to take them and make them. With that authorization, it wasn't her place to ask or even care where the monies came from and what they were for. With the right level of credentials and legitimacy of the deposits, and going through the motions of the money laundering checks, Sheri was satisfied that she had sufficiently gone through the motions to withstand any potential investigations by the Financial Services Authority. As long as she could pass the tests, then she was okay with that.

Over the years, even when in operations, she had overseen deposits from unknown sources, and there were plenty of resources out there to help, especially when you had nine zeros or more involved. The more the merrier.

She got to her desk, and coffee arrived in sync, like the service at a Michelin-starred restaurant. She was relieved of her Burberry, and her personal assistant, Amanda, was there, notebook and pen in hand, ready to take the instructions for the day and provide the daily briefing.

After the briefing, she held her staff briefing and then went on her daily walkabout, meeting and greeting, catching up with her teams, making herself visible and accessible to the teams on the floor, the folks who did the real work of the bank.

She got back to her office and the pile of paperwork for review and signature. She studied the paperwork for the two deposits and saw the newly created account name, *Barnaby*. "Barnaby?" she mused and then sanctioned the account open with her signature above the First World Bank seal.

She grabbed her coat and her bag and swooshed out of the office, heading to Flemings on Mayfair for a long, late lunch with two members of the Trakai Investment Group. It would be a good lunch. *They will be very pleased. Continue to be very pleased*, she thought as she jumped in the back of her black Mercedes S65 limousine at the front of First World Bank.

Town House
Chelsea, London, United Kingdom
7:00 p.m.

Bella was glad to be back at Lord Beecham's townhouse in Chelsea after the dustup with the two Russians. She'd just arrived with her dad and Mac, and all she wanted to do was have a cocktail and relax.

Lord Beecham met them in the foyer as they came in. She could see that he didn't look pleased. "You know what you did is all over the news," he said.

"I'm sure it is," Mitch said, hanging up his coat. He reached out and took Bella's as well. "But we didn't have any choice in the matter. We had to take them out."

"Sure you did," Lord Beecham said. "Okay then. At least it looks like you all got away clean. There's that, I guess. If you'd been identified, it could have upset our entire game plan. What the bloody hell were you thinking of?"

"We don't have a game plan, Jeffry. That's part of the fucking problem," snapped Mitch.

"Straight to the point, Mitch, as always. You are right, but let's put an end to that and get planning."

He gestured the group into the briefing room, in the former cellar of his gentleman's townhouse. There were Bob and Sam, ready and waiting. Collins and James were at the front, preparing their presentation, and then another couple of people Bella didn't recognize.

"Let me introduce you to my guests," Beecham announced. "We have my old Regiment friends, Mitch, Bob, Mac, and of course Sam, who you may have already met. We have Bella from the clandestine international operations, CIA, Colonel Collins, my right-hand man, James, my left-hand man, and may I take the opportunity to introduce my good friend from Pall Mall, Mr. James Digby from our own clandestine operations. We also have Ed from GCHQ, Prentiss from CIA special operations, and finally, our very own Andrew Bevan from MI6."

Beecham, Collins, and James went through the presentation from the day before for the benefit of the newcomers and then went on to add the latest intel gathered in the last twenty-four hours.

Mandito dead, an apparent high-level meeting with the cartel leaders in Mexico City, cleared funds at the First World Bank to the tune of $1 billion. The elections in Equatorial Guinea, the signs of political interference, foreign state meddling, the small unmarked army on the Somalian-Kenyan border with both the capability and intent of aggression.

Dankov, apparently alive and well, had apparently assassinated Conrad Yee, and given this afternoon's report from Chelsea High Street, Mitch had a price on his head. Bella thought that simply waiting for events to unfold, under the direction of Dankov, would not be the smartest of moves, and she said as much. She argued that taking the fight to Dankov was the only way to go.

On the monitors behind, it showed footage of protestors in front of a big sandstone building with iron gates and then military vehicles, water cannons, plastic bullets bouncing around, smoke grenades, riot police and soldiers beating up protestors with batons, and a brave reporter at the scene describing the mayhem behind him.

"Ladies and gentlemen." Beecham looked at Bella. "It appears that this operation has started." He pointed at the screens behind him. He turned up the volume.

CRN News Network: Election Surprise in Equatorial Guinea—6:30 p.m.

"Reporting from Malabo, Equatorial Guinea, this is Josh Penbury from CRN News Network reporting to you live.

"After decades in power and no competitive elections, this is the first time that President Mbasogo has been challenged. From early exit polls, it looks like young gun Celestino Romada Racale has not only persuaded the people to vote but convinced them that he is the right leader for the future of this oil-rich nation on the west coast of Africa.

"This is an amazing turn of events, a revolution before us, but who will ensure that the democratic decisions of the people turn into reality? There is a lot at stake here for the people who have suffered the dictatorship that has in effect raped the country and the people of Equatorial Guinea for decades, leaving them high and dry.

"It's only a matter of time, days and no longer than a couple of weeks, before we see how this plays out.

"This is Josh Penbury reporting, CRN News, Malabo."

This was at least circumstantial evidence to prove their theory. At best, it was a compelling reason to sit up, think, and work out the next best move.

"Complicated, tricky, and a downright bloody nuisance," Beecham said.

The rest of the group nodded in agreement.

Bella confirmed that the Russian peacekeeping force in the neighboring Democratic Republic of Congo was looking more and more like a force of aggression each day as the fleet built up its flotilla of men and equipment. Less and less was it looking like the fleet of a force with peaceful intentions at heart. The meeting broke up, and Bella went to her room to decompress. It had been one hell of a day. Lying on her bed, eyes to the ceiling, she thought of her mum. She missed her. With working in Washington, DC, and traveling a lot for the company, she saw her mum less often than she would have liked.

She sat up, propped a pillow behind her, and took her cell from the purse on the adjacent nightstand. Bella pressed the speed dial on her phone, and after two rings, the familiar voice of her mother was at the other end of the line.

"Bella, Bella Fonterella."

"Hello, Mum. How are you? Just calling to check in."

"Where have you been, Bella? I was worried about you."

"Here and there, Mum. What about you?" Bella knew she was being vague, but she had no choice. It made her feel awkward that she was acting a bit like Mitch had in the past.

"Oh, I have been cleaning the house. Washed the dogs this morning, did some laundry, you know, the usual. And you?"

"I'm in London with Dad. We went out for a few drinks earlier. Quaint little London pub."

"Oh. How is your father?" Angela asked pointedly.

"He's good actually, in very good form, just like his old self." Bella pictured how she had left Mitch with Mac, Beecham, and Collins, sharing a dram and laughing at stories past.

"Ask him to call me," said Angela. "When he gets a chance," she added testily.

"Do you two not talk, Mum? I think he could use it right now." She corrected herself. "I think you could both use it, right?"

"When are you heading back home, Bella?" she asked.

"Not sure. Hopefully soon. Need to see Wills. We have a big date coming up."

"Oh yes. That." Angela had already lectured Bella that at twenty-nine she was still young. She had her career, and she was still recovering from the Nikita incident.

They talked for five minutes more. Bella got the lowdown on Nonny, Zia, and her two uncles. She got caught up on some of her old school friends and the normal things they were doing with their lives—getting married to lawyers or bankers, having babies, going to the Bay Club every day of the week and the Farm Shop for evening drinks, meeting hubbies off the ferry in their immaculately bedecked size 1 and their Teslas parked outside.

It was the stereotypical Marin County life she missed, had aspired to yet also despised. She yearned for that routine and normalness, yet she couldn't think of anything worse. She thought of Wills and wondered if he was really the right one, if she indeed was ready to accept his plan of the engagement ring, settling down, having kids, and giving up her job, at least temporarily. It wasn't the first time in the past few days she felt a cold sweat come on, but this time it was for very different reasons, although equally as fearsome to Bella.

Bella said goodbye, sent her love, and hung up the phone, looking down at herself. No designer outfits for her, just a pair of tight running pants, baggy jumper over her running vest, puffer jacket, and a pair of boots. After all, is was March in London, not California.

She looked out the window at the rainy London night, her part-reflection in the window, looking beyond the skyline into herself.

Her DAD had offered counseling from the agency, an offer she had refused, but she knew there was something wrong, maybe very wrong with the level of violence she got herself involved with. Even more worrisome was the buzz and satisfaction she got from it. This was a mystery to Bella. She had known for years that Mitch had deep troubles within. He was quiet, often very quiet, happy in his own company, apart from when he with his family.

He had been through a lot in his life. He had seen death and sadness, endured pressure like no other, led men to the fire, and kept strong for them—his colleagues but also her mum and Bella. Mitch had been the protectorate to those around him for many years, and that had taken its toll.

She wondered if, other than in times of violence or whisky, she would ever see him truly happy again.

She flashed back to her childhood and being on his shoulders as they walked the edge of the Grand Canyon. She remembered the camper van, Mitch driving on the treacherous roads, Death Valley, Nevada City, having bacon sandwiches on Santa Monica Beach, just *because they could*, one of Mitch's old sayings.

She remembered all those good times, and part of her wanted them back. Mitch always told her, "Nobody said this life was going to be easy, Bella," and so far, he had been absolutely right.

Café Astros
Ostozhenka District, Moscow, Russian Federation
8:30 a.m.

Dankov and many more patriots before him had frequented Café Astros, a modest coffee shop in the Ostozhenka District, close to his apartment, close to the Kremlin and Red Square, at the heart of his motherland. Today he was meeting the leader of his motherland, a symbolic gesture, in public at this infamous and legendary café. This was as significant as any medal of honor, public recognition far beyond a ceremony. To sit down with this man at the Café Astros was truly an honor, in the company and under the watchful eye at the epicenter of Russia's undercover world.

The simple menu offered coffee, tea, a selection of Syrniki, Russian cottage cheese dumplings, savory or sweet, and vodka. Not any vodka but a fine range from Russian Standard, Shustov, Starka, and the ubiquitous Stolichnaya. After all, this was the heartland, and this was where patriots came to meet, play chess, and plan their next moves.

Each table had a chess board and a timer, with the chess pieces in a box by the side. There were only a dozen tables inside the stark and dark interior, the menu board, and ladies' and men's toilets. That was it. Only in recent years had women been seen in Café Astros, as previously it was reserved for the business of men.

Viktoria Saparov was one of the pioneers who had changed that, and in her wake, there were several very promising additions to their ranks, appreciated by most, Dankov included.

While his security detail sat in the black SUV on the curbside, Dankov chose to sit outside, despite the cold March morning. The sun was out in the clear blue sky, and between the patio heater, his coffee, Syrniki, and the vodka, he was warm enough.

Despite those comforts, he had been through a lot. His father had been through more during the siege of Leningrad before him. He felt a sense of great pride, and the cold just served as a reminder of the sacrifices that had been made before him. Losing his leg was a sacrifice but nothing compared with those brave comrades on the frozen tundra for nearly four years. His scars on the right side of his face, healed but sensitive, were a welcome reminder of the pain and served to cut an even more impressive and recognizable figure as he navigated the streets and the corridors of the heartland, wearing his medal of honor for all to see. Dmitri Dankov needed no introduction before the incident and certainly needed no introduction now. Dankov was a comrade, a patriot, and a hero.

Café Astros was quiet that morning, largely due to the man he was meeting and the security clearing of the cafe. There would be no casual passersby, no walk-ins, no cameras, no press. Just Putin, Dankov, and the security detail inside and out. They were probably in the safest place in Russia at that moment.

The man in the big blue overcoat sat down before him. Dankov made the feigned courtesy of standing up.

"Pozhaluysta, pozhaluysta, syad'te." (Please, please, sit down.) "You should rest those weary legs of yours," he said with a glint of dark humor.

"Very funny, Vlad."

Both men laughed.

A waiter hurried over, took their order, and left. He returned a short time later with their coffee, a small plate of Syrniki, and a shot of Russian Standard each. They clinked glasses, made a toast, and downed the vodka, "V Imperiyu." (To the Empire.)

Although they had enjoyed many games together in the past, Dankov knew that they would not be playing chess today. There were more pressing things ahead.

"Our small army is ready to move," Dankov said, keeping his voice low, though he was certain they weren't being monitored. "And so are the troops in Congo. The boots on the ground in Malabo are stirring things up as well. All the pieces of the puzzle are coming together, just like we planned."

Putin nodded. "I love it when a plan comes together, like they say on American TV."

Dankov emptied his glass. He waved the waiter over and ordered another round. He exchanged small talk with his master. Another two glasses arrived, filled with Russian Standard, and they snapped them back in a synchronized display.

Dankov continued his briefing, letting Putin know that the plan to assassinate Yee, the Dog, had come off without a hitch, except that his wife and child had been collateral damage. "Shit happens," he said.

Putin nodded, his face grim. "And what about Mitch? My people say he's still alive and kicking and that he took out two of our operatives the other day."

"If they didn't act like idiots, they'd still be alive," Dankov said. He paused, lost in thought, and then said, "Mitch is a deadster, and so are his wife and daughter. But we can bide our time with this if we want to. I'm in no hurry."

Putin ate a dumpling and said, "Suit yourself. Just know, comrade, that you have the full resources of my government behind you in this. The attempt on your life will be avenged."

"I want him to suffer like I suffered," Dankov said, his hand instinctively going to his missing leg, touching the prosthetic instead. "I will make sure he does. First, I'll kill his daughter ... real slow and on video. Then I'll do the same with his wifey poo. He'll know it's me behind it, and he'll go insane with rage. That's when we can take him down."

Putin smiled. "Sounds like a plan to me," he said. "Bianca did a masterful job in bringing the cartels together. She was a good find, Dimitri, a very good find."

"Thank you, Vlad. I think so too."

"We need to give Bianca whatever support she needs." He looked Dankov in the eye. "We need to make sure that the cartels are completely committed and don't change their minds. At any time."

"I am going to send sleepers to keep an eye on things and protect our interests."

The two nodded in unison.

"What reaction do you think we will get when we own Malabo?" Putin asked.

"We can stay there as long as we look like peacekeepers, and by the time it's all settled and we install our Presidential Six, pulling the strings of Racale's newly formed government, we will be good. Racale gets what he wants, we get what we want, everyone is happy."

"Then I think we should set the plan in motion." He paused, leaned closer to Dankov, and said, "Dmitri, you are a very good friend. You have been a very special patriot to our country. I wanted you to know how much I value your operations. I wanted to give you a gift."

Dankov interrupted his old friend politely with a hand gesture.

"Seriously, I don't ask or want for anything. You know that."

"Dmitri, I am going to present you with the highest honor of this nation. I am going to present you with your Gold Star."

To be offered the Hero of the Russian Federation, the Gold Star, the highest honorary title in the land, made even Dankov step back with surprise and a glint of teary pride. "I can't accept this," he said. "I don't deserve it."

"Of course you do! Don't be ridiculous. This honor is the least that you deserve. Thank you on behalf of the entire Russian people for all that you have done and for all that you will do in the future. The very near future, I might add."

They stood up, embraced, and at the same time said, "Spasibo Brat," patting each other on the back as they embraced like brothers.

19
HAUNTS

Malabo
Equatorial Guinea, West Africa
5:20 p.m.

THE AIR FRANCE FLIGHT 958, Boeing 777, touched down at Malabo International Airport. Bob was least pleased to be back in this territory that he had left and swapped out for a better life. But he was here again and had a job to do.

The team had discovered a complex web of deceit, and even Bob in his extremes of cynicism found it all hard to believe.

As he arrived at passport control, his visa, courtesy of the BGPC, still valid, the man behind the counter scanned Bob's passport, looked at the screen, looked at Bob, and said, "Purpose of travel to Equatorial Guinea?"

Bob just looked at him, pan-faced. "I have come to revel in the delights of your country!" Bob said sarcastically, his poor attempt of humor and sarcasm lost on the passport control officer.

"Where are you staying?" asked the officer.

"The Shangri La." Bob grimaced. The officer looked puzzled. "The Hilton." Bob smiled.

The passport security officer didn't look too impressed as he stamped his passport and visa and ushered him through.

"Fucking idiot," Bob muttered under his breath. "Fucking shithole."

He sailed through customs with his black backpack, grabbed a cab, and headed out on the less-than-five-mile, fifteen-minute ride to downtown Malabo and to the Malabo Hilton—at least some standard of oasis in this shithole. The cab pulled up in front of the hotel. Bob paid, took his backpack from the seat beside him, and strolled into the lobby. Bob quickly surveyed the area. He figured the government had him on a watch list and that he'd have at least a tail or two while he was there.

One big fat local, reading the *London Times* in his ill-fitting, hand-me-down suit with large sweat patches under the armpits, looking like a character from a stereotypical Bond film, was of little interest or perceived risk.

Another pair, with designer sunglasses, sat at a coffee table—no coffee, no nothing, just sat there waiting. They didn't strike him as too much of a threat either. "Fucking amateurs," he muttered.

Then there was one man on his own—smart suit, slender, athletic, North African, Algerian demeanor, BGPC watch on his left wrist. Bob was okay with this, his old firm keeping an eye on him.

He strode to the elevator and went to his suite. Bob had made good money with BGPC. The bonus he had received on the $150 million retrieval took care of that, and with a good top-up salary with Grace & Co, Bob didn't need to scrimp. That said, the suites in this place were hardly the Ritz, he reminded himself as he dumped his black backpack on the bed and checked out the room. He went across to the window to the view of Malabo, a view he had hoped he would never see again.

Feeling restless and a little jet-lagged, he went down to the bar. He ordered some food and had a couple of beers and then a series of the boring Hilton range of whisky before heading to his room for the night.

He signed the tab, headed to the elevators, and went to his room. His phone buzzed, a text message: "Welcome Home, Mr. Bob." He knew exactly who it was from, or at least one of the potential six people it was from.

In the morning, he would go to the BGPC headquarters to get up to speed and see his old friends, including the Legionnaire, Hamza Malik.

Hosingow
Somalia, East Africa
2:00 a.m.

Boris Latminko sat on the front line of the HC-130. Not like that of a civilian ride, this was a little more basic. It had a triple row of canvass seats at the front, twelve by six, and the rest of the crew reclined in the hammocks strewn down the middle of the aircraft, with their gear on each side.

The HC-130 rumbled and bounced, creaked and yearned to make it from the ground into the air. Not some first-class seated affair but an array of hammock-like strappings, with the cargo behind, a collection of mainly US military hardware and enough munitions to sink a ship or take over a small country.

As they rumbled along the airstrip, Latminko closed his eyes as he played out each bump and turn, thinking through the unimaginable eventualities of this big, overburdened beast, rumbling through the dust and eventually making it airborne before the runway ran out.

He felt every bump, sway, surge, and accumulation and the eventual but tentative signals of flight. He could feel the loft of the speed and the aeronautics taking hold slowly, then eventually the pilot's thrust, a combination of air, speed, and loft taking them into the air, followed by the shudder of the skeleton holding the HC-130 together. "Fucking Americans!"

The HC-130 climbed and steadied out at twelve thousand feet, sufficient to be below the great commercial jet highway. Radio contact confirmed that the other two were successfully up in the air and on their way.

Once the plane had levelled out, at altitude, like a big growling bear, Latminko inspected his troops, checking in, confirming their understanding of their part in the intricate symphony he was about to unleash. Just like a conductor with his orchestra.

With his nondescript black camouflage, intricate webbing that concealed his water bottle, first aid kit, compass, ubiquitous rounds for various armaments, no insignia or rank showing, Latminko was still clearly the boss. It was obvious to any observer.

Satisfied, he went back to his seat, sat down, and looked inside his webbing for his most important stash, his Russian Standard vodka.

His troops were on their way. And they were ready.

He sat looking ahead, hearing, feeling the HC-130 engines rumble away, whine in their circular motion, like a repeated throbbing, turning into a pattern after a while.

They would land at a temporary Russian military airstrip, refuel, and wait for the final signal for the short hop into Equatorial Guinea. Hopefully, they wouldn't be on hold there for too long. The boys would get itchy and irritated, and so would Latminko.

The HC-130 suddenly rocked, shook, shifted sideways, and then started to rattle as the turbulence outside bounced them around like a Meccano set in the wind.

Boris took another slurp of his vodka, closed his eyes, and just listened to the rattling, imagining the rivets and the bolts working loose. He played out a scenario in his head of what they would do if they went down.

He opened an eye like a big brown bear as the copilot approached him with the details of the flight path, cruising altitude, speed, fuel, and estimated time to touch down.

Boris grunted his approval and sat back, ready for a snooze. There was nothing else to do. Not yet.

Hours Later
Hosingow
Somalia, East Africa
6:45 a.m.

The British Army Air Corps Westland Gazelle hummed through the East African early-morning sky like a hummingbird quietly and unassumingly about its mission, close to the ground, hedgehopping, although in this part of the world, there were not too many hedges to hop.

Bella sat in the back with three other operatives from the CIA, plus Mitch and Mac, heading out to check the launch pad and verify the reports of Latminko's assault force.

The Gazelle, with the rear doors open, offered a great view of the savanna, and despite its relatively quiet hum, it was powerful enough to stir the elephants, giraffes, and herds of zebras and wildebeest below them in the early-morning African plains.

It felt more like a safari than the serious mission they were on—to verify their theory that an aggressive invading force was using this as a launch pad to take over a sovereign state, in this case, Equatorial Guinea.

Bella looked over at her father and saw a glint in his eye that she hadn't seen for some time.

Times had changed, their relationship had changed, and Bella was no longer the little girl who needed Mitch's protection. He had taught her well. Maybe too well. She had grown a liking for this stuff, as Mitch had before her. Bella was reflective but proud. It had been a journey, but she was pleased with where they both were, at least for the time being.

The big orange sun started to glimmer and shimmer across the golden, sun-scorched earth. Bella couldn't get the song out of her mind, "Golden Brown," for all the implications. She found it on her phone and plugged it into the in-craft headset system.

She knew that both Mitch and Mac would like this tune, but she wasn't sure about her CIA cousins. Bella had grown up listening to Mitch's music collection. She looked back at them both with pride and more. *For the boys*, she thought.

They sailed together through the early-morning golden sky, looking out over the savannah, the animals, and the herds, and as they neared their intended location, the music stopped, and the aircrew got a lot more serious.

As the pilot compared the latest satellite images and the radar, he announced to the passengers, "They've gone."

"Looks like they have bugged out."

"Recently. Maybe in the last couple of hours."

They neared what was obviously a former compound with the footprints of the soldiers, scars on the land where the tents used to be, still visible, the evidence of the tracks of the HC-130 still fresh, vehicle tracks still evident, and the scuffle of boots still on display. As the Gazelle landed, there were further signs of fire pits extinguished and piles of garbage smoldering where they had been incinerated, eventually dissolving into nothing, standard procedures to remove as much evidence before you leave. This was a party of four hundred men and machines, so it didn't disappear overnight. *At least a few days*, Bella thought.

Although somewhat relieved, Bella knew their mission wasn't wasted. Having boots on the ground and confirmation of their departure was very useful.

Although the HC-130s had a four-thousand-mile range, if they were indeed headed to Equatorial Guinea, then they were heading to a pit stop before making their final move.

Bella looked at the team and stated, "DRC is my bet," referring to the Democratic Republic of Congo, right next door to Equatorial Guinea and in effect controlled by the Russians.

She made a call, checked ahead, and her assessment was confirmed. Affirmative. "They are on their way."

Later That Night
Kinshasa
Democratic Republic of Congo, Central Africa
11:00 p.m.

Bella, Mitch, and Mac touched down at the N'djili International Airport just outside Kinshasa, the capital of the DRC. On the flight, they had been receiving intel of the three HC-130s making their passage from Somalia to the remote Russian airstrip, and as they landed, the reports were that they were still there.

It had been a long day. The three sat in the Toyota Landcruiser from the airport to their hotel.

"Fucking genius if you think about it," Mac said.

"What? Invade a country while the world sleeps?" Bella asked.

"Exactly. What can the world actually do about it?" Mitch asked.

"Not much if there is nothing to see, right? From the outside looking in, this is just a tin-pot dictatorship coming to its end, and the Russians just happen to be in the neighborhood, preventing the situation from becoming a blood bath," Bella said, connecting all the dots.

"Like I say, fucking genius," Mac repeated.

"Wish there was something we could do," Bella said, "but right now we have to let the situation play out. See what happens next."

CRN News Network: President Challenges Election Results—6:00 p.m.

"Reporting from Malabo, Equatorial Guinea, this is Josh Penbury from CRN News Network reporting to you live.

"The election results are now out. Initial reports claim that Celestino Romada Racale has won the popular vote, but in developments in the last few hours, President Mbasogo is claiming election rigging and fraud and that the election is void.

"In a statement from Government House, President Mbasogo's spokesman announced that the government was not recognizing the legitimacy of the election process and would hold a reelection in the coming few months.

"In the meantime, clashes are taking place across Malabo between Racale's Social Democratic Party supporters in high tension with government police and security forces.

"In a statement from Racale earlier today, he stated,

"'I am not surprised at the government's reaction, and despite a clear and decisive win and a loss of confidence in the current oppressive regime, the current government continues to cling to our nation's assets and the wealth of the people.'

"'Today, the people have voted, and as the world watches, they will support the freedom of people and the principles of democracy.'

"The next few days will be critical to understanding how this story will unfold.

"This is Josh Penbury reporting, CRN News, Malabo."

The Government Building
Malabo, Equatorial Guinea
10:30 a.m.

President Mbasogo sat in his office waiting for the calls. He knew they were coming. He had seen it play out before, on the news in Libya and more recently in Venezuela. This wasn't the first time and likely not the last, he thought. But could he survive? That was the question on his mind.

The bank of flat screens on his wall were playing the news from around the world and the various feeds documenting and following the Equatorial Guinea situation as it unfolded. Mbasogo closed his eyes, just wishing it would all go away.

In his Savile Row suit, his Dunhill shoes, his ironic Trump tie, and his sparkling gold Rolex, Mbasogo was dressed in his work clothes, ready to take the calls from other world leaders.

He himself was a world leader. He had earned that right from the day he removed his uncle from office. His assassination was of course handled by others, but the ultimate outcome was the same. He had ruled the country ever since, elevating its oil production to make it among the top handful of oil-producing nations in Africa. Sure, there was corruption. Sure, the place wasn't perfect. Where in Africa was? Exactly. He nodded to himself as he opened his eyes and looked to the bank of screens, then to the big gold phone on his desk.

This office, the job, the trimmings were his right. Why should it be okay for some upstart to come on to the scene, stirring trouble, wrestling for his crown?

Mbasogo also knew that Racale wasn't alone. He knew that there were outside powers at play. He knew that simply silencing Racale could have even more serious consequences. He had been tempted. He was tempted now. But that might mean civil war and little or no backdoor exit for him.

Why were these people meddling in his kingdom? He banged his oversized fist on his mahogany desk.

What would he say to them when they called? Mind their own business? Refuse their requests to step down? Not even answer their calls?

He knew that none of the above would be a good idea.

They were probably on their phones right now, rallying their support. It would start with the US calling Spain first, out of courtesy. Then the UK, then France, Italy, then South Africa, probably Morocco, the Australians, New Zealanders, the Canadians.

They were going to ask him to stand down. What would he say? He didn't have much choice.

He had his place in Belgravia, London. Who in corrupt West Africa didn't? He also had properties all over the world, but London would be his base. He had already arranged for bank transfers to take place, so he had plenty of accessible liquid cash on hand. He might need it for a very long time, he had surmised.

He had sent cash over and placed it in his secure safe in London, just in case assets got frozen, although going peacefully, he might be able to negotiate a release, assets intact. That was probably his best option. He knew that, but it was hard to give up, not just because of the material things and the power but also the humiliation. He had to leave on his own terms and with his pride and head held high.

How would he, how could he deal with his enemies? He knew that he had accumulated many in this incredibly competitive, dog-eat-dog nation. Did he have time? Did he have the means? There was always his personal security detail—the most loyal, the best trained, the best paid—but even they would have their loyalty tested over the next few days.

He would deal with that later. The phone rang before him. He stared at it as if surprised and took a deep breath. The familiar female voice of his assistant was on the line.

"Mr. President, I have the president of the United States on the line."

Mbasogo looked out the window, paused for a moment, returned his gaze to the room, and said, "Put him through."

CRN News Network: The USA and Other
Nations Recognize Interim Leader—6:00 p.m.

"Reporting from Malabo, Equatorial Guinea, this is Josh Penbury from CRN News Network reporting to you live.

"In the latest development, like events that took place in Venezuela, the US government has announced its support of and recognition that Celestino Romada Racale is acknowledged internationally as Equatorial Guinea's new interim leader. Fourteen countries have followed suit, supporting Racale, putting pressure on Mbasogo to step down.

"In reaction, President Mbasogo has called a national emergency and mobilized his military in the capital, Malabo.

"Clashes between protestors and security forces have increased and gained in terms of violence with awful scenes of brutality on the streets.

"Equatorial Guinea is just the latest example of where the people have made moves to remove oppressive regimes and where those regimes resist at all costs.

"President Mbasogo has ordered the removal of all diplomats from the United States, United Kingdom, Australia, South Africa, and ten other countries within the next seventy-two hours.

"This is Josh Penbury reporting, CRN News, Malabo."

20
PINSTRIPES AND POPPIES

Whitehall
London, United Kingdom
7:55 a.m.

JAMES DIGBY DRESSED IN HIS red cavalry twill trousers, Church's brogues, Thomas Pink shirt, and checked sports jacket with elbow patches and a dog-eared poppy on his left lapel. He liked to prolong the British Legion campaign for old soldiers, and with the pink dress shirt, he looked quite the officer, an army officer, a Blues and Royals, Household Cavalry officer. Or at least a former one.

He got to the front of the big white building in the heart of Whitehall, its big black door and brass knocker. He looked at his Bremont watch. "Right on time." He walked into the front reception and up to the briefing room on the second floor.

His job was so much more exciting when something was happening. The days of waiting and watching, filling in paperwork were just as dull as dishwater. James Digby liked the exciting stuff.

He got to the briefing room door, stopped and listened, then politely but firmly knocked. "Come in," came the distinctive bellow, and in walked Digby to an esteemed audience and the highest-ranking military officers and diplomats in the country.

"Morning, gentlemen," Digby said in typical Cavalry fashion as he sat down and pulled in his chair in the company of his audience, the most senior ranks of the navy, the Royal Airforce, and the army, in addition to the head of MI6, the home secretary and foreign secretary representing Her Majesty's government.

The wood-paneled room had a presentation screen at the front, appearing out of the panels with the simple words Intelligence Briefing. Digby started the story, condensing it to the salient facts and distilling it into a fifteen-minute brief. These men didn't have time as a luxury; in their worlds, time was finite and precious, and decisions needed to be made. Procrastination wasn't on the agenda.

Digby finished his pitch and surveyed the audience, trying to work out how well he had done or otherwise. It was difficult to tell from his audience of seasoned military, service, and political backgrounds.

"Questions?"

Guy, the man in the combats representing the army, said, "Great briefing, Digby, but how much of this story is corroborated?"

"Yep, understood. We have evidence that supports every detail of the tale you just heard, at least as far as we know," responded Digby.

"As far as you know? What the hell does that mean?" said the head of the air force.

Digby was ready, anticipating the question. "Yes, sir! We have verification of every facet of the story I just told you, with varying degrees of certainty from evidence gathered via satellite, local teams on the ground, known events, and observations. The collection of the facts, despite the varying levels of reliability, together point to this: a Russian-backed rebellion of sorts is going to result in Russia taking control of the sixth-largest oil nation on the African continent. This is potentially a new model for inter-sovereign aggression and a means to take control under the radar, so to speak."

"And the Russians, Mexicans?" asked the head of the navy.

"A marriage in paradise. Mandito International wants out of drugs, wants to exercise its more lucrative activities with an aligned and collaborative cartel group. In their pursuit of cash businesses, you probably saw that they just added GroMart to their portfolio and now a 420,000-barrel-a-day oil cash flow. Makes sense, right?"

"This Bianca Blanca sounds like a trip," said the man in the blue suit from the MI6. "We could do with some of her."

"So, how close is Putin to all this?" asked the foreign secretary.

"We think he is pretty close, even the executive sponsor. He met with Dmitri Dankov recently at a coffee shop in Moscow. We believe to give him the order to proceed."

"Where is this so-called rebel force now?" asked the home secretary.

"Yes, sir. They apparently left Somalia very early Monday morning, and they are sitting waiting in the Democratic Republic of Congo to refuel and head to Equatorial Guinea from there. This is what our intel tells us, and with the patterns of behavior and circumstances, we believe that their target is EG."

"So," said the foreign secretary, "the Russians along with the Mexican cartels club together to fund a rebel force to invade an oil-rich country, on the basis of improving their cash flow, then conveniently, their well-placed peacekeeping force right next door happens to roll in and take over a country on the African continent?"

"Yes, sir. That's it in a nutshell," replied Digby.

"Fucking genius!" replied the foreign secretary. "You couldn't make this stuff up!"

"Sounds like something we would do one hundred and fifty years ago," added the head of the army.

The group nodded, upward smiles, hints of laughs and agreement. The humor of the statement was not lost.

"So, Digby, what do you need from us?" asked the home secretary.

"Nothing, sir. Just wanted to make sure you were fully briefed and that No. 10 was fully aware of this unfolding story when the Russian Federation hoists their flag in Malabo in the coming days."

The head of the army commented, "It sounds like a rerun of that Wonga Coup a few years back—Calil, Mark Thatcher, Simon Mann, and company."

"Well, Digby, keep us informed. I will brief the prime minister this afternoon. Thanks for coming in."

That was Digby's signal that he was dismissed. He decided to head off to the Cavalry Club for a late brunch and catch up, where he read the news of Eli Calil, who was soft-spoken, well connected, and intensely disliked by his former Wonga Coup colleagues.

Digby knew of him, in fact had met him in passing at a mutual acquaintance's wedding out in Henley a few years back. Calil's business dealings helped spread corruption and misrule across Africa, and he was named as one of the plotters and funders of the Wonga Coup—a plot to take over Equatorial Guinea and gain access to its abundance of black gold—in collaboration with Simon Mann, an old Etonian and former SAS officer, and a band of mercenaries.

Digby arrived at the club, looked over his newspaper, took a sip of his tea, and looked out of the window across London.

CRN News Network: Riots and Violence in Equatorial Guinea—6:00 p.m.

"Reporting from Malabo, Equatorial Guinea, this is Josh Penbury from CRN News Network reporting to you live.

"The past twenty-four hours have been the most violent yet, with an escalation of demonstrations and clashes between government forces and the people. Crowds of many tens of thousands have gathered and are now arming themselves with anything they can find. There have been reports of gunshots from the protestors and reports of injuries and deaths on both sides, with the government reciting the numbers.

"Racale is calling the people to a peaceful solution, but the level of brutality on the streets is growing, as is the resistance from the people.

"This is like a pressure cooker about to go off, and something will have to give.

"This is Josh Penbury reporting, CRN News, Malabo."

21
COMPOUND INTEREST

British Gas & Pipeline Corporation
Malabo, Equatorial Guinea, West Africa
7:30 a.m.

BIG BAD BOB HAD ARRANGED to meet with Hamza Malik at the shiny new office building in the BGPC complex just outside of the city. As he strolled across the dusty and dirty compound, he remembered the many times he had made that journey before.

At that time of the morning, Malabo was at its most pleasant. It had been a hot, humid night at the Hilton. Bob hadn't slept much, but he was relieved to be in the morning sunshine before it reached its full humid heat. A cool slight breeze blowing from the west was just enough to kick up the dust, occasionally creating little dancing whirring dervishes rising from the ground.

He knew exactly where he was going, the new offices, as he had been fundamental in their design—functional and practical, solid and secure, with an underground bunker built in too. They had designed the building not just as an office but as a safe haven if this place ever kicked off, which, given the stability of Equatorial Guinea or the lack thereof, was always a distinct possibility.

Around the perimeter, there was a combination of contract blocks and double-layered barbed wire, making it impossible for a vehicle to get through anywhere but the front door, and almost impossible for anyone on foot.

Bob noticed that they had been busy, and the camera upgrade was now installed as well as the observation towers with the mounted M2 .50-caliber machine guns capable of firing and aiming from the control room, spitting out over twelve hundred rounds a minute. With six of these placed around the compound and with their mile-plus range, they were a substantial deterrent for any advancing force, whoever they were.

In the yard, he also noticed a collection of mobility vehicles from half-tracks to all-terrain buggies, motorcycles, and a collection of a dozen Mi-24 transport and attack helicopters. He looked back at the main gate and confirmed the enhanced security personnel.

As Bob approached the familiar figure of Hamza Malik, he held out a hand.

"Expecting visitors, my friend? What the fuck is going on here?"

Malik inspected his feet for a moment, looked up at Bob, and just shrugged. "You, of course, Mr. Bob, a VIP visiting our humble abode." He accentuated the P with a somewhat sarcastic and provocative tone, almost a hiss.

Bob held himself, recognizing that all in the garden here was not rosy.

"What the fuck is up with you, Hamza?" he said, looking deep into Malik's soul like only a man who had seen both sides of life could.

Malik looked down at the floor and then to the right to the skyline.

"What the fuck's wrong, Hamza?" Bob could see the tension in Malik's face, like a child holding on to a big secret, full of resentment, full of anger, and full of pride.

Bob wanted to stay outside. Whatever was wrong, it was best kept from the audio monitoring and recording in the building. Whatever it was, it was best to discuss, albeit in front of the ubiquitous cameras, out of earshot of any device.

"They have my sister and her kids," Malik said, tight, angry, and hissing like a cobra.

"Who has your sister?" Bob probed.

"Those fuckers you catapulted out of the country to London. They have paid a lot of interest lately and had me turn this place into a fortress."

"For the rebel force?" Bob asked.

Bob could see Malik weighing him. He knew he was taller at six foot three. He kept himself fit and toned, was often referred to as bearlike, with his dark brown hair, now slightly graying at the temples. Bob saw something in Malik's eyes like a pang of recognition of a memory from the past, a penny dropping, a realization of some kind.

"How do you know about any rebel force?"

Bob just stared back. Face blank. "They're on their way here. I know that much. Refueling in DRC as we speak." Bob stated what he knew to be true. "Where do they have your sister? In Paris?"

"Yes. They have her holed up at her apartment."

"We will sort that out. Don't worry."

"They had me go out to Somalia last week. To go and meet them."

"Who?"

"The fucking Russians!" snapped Malik, showing further signs of irritation and aggression. "A small army camped out on the Somalia-Kenya border. Russians, no ranks, insignia, and official Russian mercenaries. The Presidential Six are at the center of this."

"The Presidential Six?"

"That's what they are calling them. Backers of Racale. Funders of the revolution. The Presidential Six that will be pulling strings here soon."

"Yep, but who's pulling *their* strings is the question," Bob said. "Come on. Let's get a crew to your sister's and get that sorted out." Bob patted Hamza on the back and reassured him that all would be good.

Malik looked at Bob. "You are always so damn fucking right, Bob. But you've been doing this for a long time."

Malabo Investment Enterprise
Malabo, Equatorial Guinea, West Africa
11:30 a.m.

The leader of the Presidential Six tried to control his anger about the situation. He gazed around the room at his five companions, noting that they made quite a sight. None of them were particularly attractive. He knew he was the most overweight, with his shirt threatening to pop its buttons and unleash the mass behind it. He looked at the gold sovereign ring on his little finger, his hands small in proportion to his supersized body. He didn't care. Money took care of everything, even the ugly. But money without power was less appealing, and that was exactly what it sounded like Dimitri Dankov was promising them.

The conversation paused for a moment, and then Dankov's voice came through the speakerphone. "You have to understand our position," he said. "We have made all the arrangements, and we must maintain control at all costs if this is to work out as planned."

"We want the plan to work out too," the leader said. "We just don't want our balls cut off politically." The leader picked up his glass of bourbon, took a sip, swallowed, and felt the warmth of the alcohol in his ample stomach. "I want you to know I feel—we feel—betrayed. We will put an end to your army. We will stop them from entering our nation. We will not tolerate this piracy. Do you understand, Dankov?"

Dankov laughed. "And you will stop us with what? A peashooter? That's about all the firepower you have. Look, you'll get paid for your troubles in all this. I promise you that, and I keep my promises."

Yeah, sure, the leader thought. *When pigs fly.*

"I know you do," the leader said, hoping to placate Dankov, or at least keep him from going back on the payments. "I guess we have no other choice but to let this play out."

"No, you don't," Dankov said. "No choice at all, in fact."

A Remote Airstrip
Sankuru Province
Democratic Republic of Congo
10:00 p.m.

The big Russian, Boris Latminko, was irritated at the wait, but he was always irritated. They had received their orders from Dankov to proceed, and they were all ready to go. Within twenty minutes of the phone call, Boris had the three HC-130 aircraft loaded and rumbling down the temporary and very bumpy runway.

Boris once again closed his eyes, took a gulp of his Russian Standard vodka, and started replaying the plans in his mind.

Each of the three HC-130s had one hundred of his men ready to parachute just outside of the city center to three different drop zones and rendezvous points. They would synchronize the drop, and in less than four minutes, the three hundred soldiers would be on the way down to their drop zones, and the three HC-130s, ten minutes later, would be landing at the Malabo International Airport, no permission to land, no stack time, just straight into the land. They knew that they had a ten-minute window between midnight and twelve thirty to get down and out between arrivals, mobilize the remaining troops and vehicles, and take out the lightly protected airport, lightly protected by a poorly trained and poorly equipped defense.

This had the hallmarks of a walk in the park, but Latminko knew he should never make assumptions or take anything for granted—and always expect the worst.

The night was perfect. Clear skies, no wind. The team, packaged up, saw the prewarning, yellow lights come on, their signal to line up for their silent jump into the darkness.

Boris, at the front of the line and in full *game on* mode, got ready to help the dispatcher signal the boys for their jump. Careful positioning and altitude adjustments allowed them to be ready precisely at jump time.

With the signal from the pilot, the dispatcher was ready, and the line shuffled like a line of penguins ready to go. Green, go, go, go. Green, go, go, go. The double line, two at a time, jumped into the darkness, and within four minutes, they were all gone.

That meant thirty minutes to touchdown, and the remaining team manned the array of vehicles in readiness for the prestart and landing so that as soon as the H-130s came to a halt, they would be out the back of the aircraft, heading to their target destinations, and taking out the defenses that existed.

Given the firepower and the sheer imbalance of training, experience, and quality of personnel, Latminko wasn't expecting a problem, but in this game of life or death, there was no place for unnecessary risks.

Breaking News: CRN News Network: Takeover Coup in Equatorial Guinea

"Josh Penbury, CRN News Network, reporting from Malabo, Equatorial Guinea.

"We have just received news that multiple aircraft have landed at Malabo Airport and that a land assault has started with gunshots, missiles, and explosions coming from the airport just an hour ago.

"You could see the explosions in the night sky as the battle progressed for less than twenty minutes, followed by a steady stream of military vehicles rolling into the city, taking on government forces. There were many dozens of soldiers seen parachuting into the city, with the drop zone being the Government Building.

"The unknown force with what seems like US military equipment bears no insignia from where they are from, but one thing that we do know is that these soldiers are professionals. Very well trained and very well armed. Even the Presidential Guard are no match for these invaders.

"It seems only a matter of time before the Government Building is taken.

"This is Josh Penbury reporting, CRN News, Malabo."

22
PARIS

Apartment 11, Bourgogne Building
Paris, France
2:30 a.m.

BELLA GLANCED AT THE SEVEN men who were with
her in the narrow hallway outside the door of their target's
apartment in Paris. They were all dressed in black from the
tips of their boots to their black gasmasks and balaclavas.
Each carried a Heckler & Koch MP5 tightly pulled into their
shoulders. The lead man had a sledgehammer battering ram
for the door. The second had stun grenades and gas, and the
remainder were ready to go with an imprint in their heads of
the layout of the apartment and from the heat maps showing
where the targets and the assets were likely to be. This would
be an operation of surprise, full force, and accuracy.

As this was her first mission in the field, she naturally
felt nervous, not because she was scared of a shootout but
because she didn't want to screw up in front of the guys,

including her father, who was with them in a supporting role, not as team leader.

Although English wasn't most of the group's native tongue, the orders were short, sharp, and simple and didn't need much interpretation or translation. It was better that way, one common assault language, English in this case. She had recalled her studies of the USSR forces and how their multiple languages had impeded their efficiency, and lost translations or flat misunderstandings led to errors and in some cases defeat. A common language was the most efficient and effective.

Bella heard the orders over her earpiece telling the team to go. Instantly, the rammer splintered the door of the apartment. The next man tossed the stun grenades and gas bombs. Deafening bangs shook the building as the grenades went off. She felt the concussive wave wash over her as she dashed into the apartment behind Mitch, her gun at the ready, the smoke green in her night vision goggles. The team fanned out, clearing each room one by one.

"Clear!"

"Clear!" she shouted as she emerged from an empty bedroom after checking the closets, even looking under the bed. She rushed into the next room, the room where the heat map imagery indicated the kidnappers were. She kicked open the door, was first in, and confirmed no children or females. In the split seconds that passed as she processed the scene, she saw two men turn on her, their guns raised. It had been just under a minute since the breach of the apartment, but those guys were ready and loaded for bear. The men fired all at once. Bella leaped to the side, firing as she flew through the air. She felt bullets pass close by her head. Screaming, she unloaded on the men on full automatic. Blood, brain, bones, flesh … the scene was one of complete carnage. And Bella was in her full element, like a lioness on the hunt in the great Serengeti. As she mowed the men down, she recognized one of them, and her anger and rage flared to white hot as she riddled her assailants with almost hysterical zest. Suddenly, a third man jumped out of the walk-in wardrobe, momentarily startling Bella.

"You're dead!" the man screamed as he leveled his AK-47 and opened up on her. "You stupid little cow! You're dead!"

Bella reacted fast, hitting the deck and rolling off to the side while keeping up a steady return fire. She was vaguely aware of shouts and bootsteps pounding outside the room and getting closer … closer …

The third man had her pinned down. He emptied his magazine and quickly jammed another clip into the rifle. As he opened up again, wood splintered around Bella. Every second seemed like forever.

"Die! Die, you son of a bitch!" she screamed, pivoting to the left, and then standing right up, her gun blazing.

The assailant seemed surprised that she'd expose herself like that, and for a second he hesitated. Those seconds were all Bella needed. She went for the head as she fired from the hip, sending a spray of rounds pounding into the man's face, disintegrating it entirely. Indeed, the man's head disappeared into a cloud of pink mist.

"Fuckin' asshole," she said.

"You sure did him good," Mitch said from the doorway. He had a slight smile on his face, as if he'd just seen a part of her that he didn't know existed. In that flash of a moment, it occurred to her that nobody had seen this side of her.

"Yeah, well, he deserved it."

"Yes, he did," Mitch said.

The gunfight had lasted less than two minutes, and she'd offed three guys. She'd never killed someone before, and the shock of it was already starting to kick in. Sure, she was a tough lady, hard as nails in some respects, but she was still human, and she was still new to the field.

"You okay, Bella?" Mitch asked, walking over to her and looking her in the eye.

Suddenly, Bella felt like she wanted to cry. She pushed the emotions away, bit her lower lip, and said, "I'm fine, Dad. Just a close one. That's all."

Mitch surveyed the dead. "Looks like they didn't know what hit 'em."

Bella laughed, albeit a short, forced laugh. "Lotta good all their security did them. They thought they got away clean. Well, I got news for you guys ..."

"Come on," Mitch said. "Let's get outta here."

Just then, sirens began wailing in the distance. In a matter of minutes, the entire neighborhood would be crawling with bobbies. Operation complete, they jumped on the bus with the other operatives back to the Parisian headquarters of the Commandement des Opérations Spéciales to hand back their hardware and for a debrief on that night's events.

Mitch and Mac sat next to each other, and Bella took the row behind them on the plain black Citroen bus, watching out of the window as they sped through the early-morning Parisian streets.

She knew that the more money that was involved, the higher levels of greed, oil, international players, Russians, cartels, and the corrupt Equatorial Guineans. The stakes got higher and infinitely more dangerous.

The news was coming through on the demise of Equatorial Guinea and what seemed a perfectly masterminded coup under the guise of peacekeeping, and she knew there wasn't much the world could do about it apart from standing by and watching. After all, the world was asleep to it; it was only their small group who had pieced the puzzle together, but it was too late to do anything about it.

The trauma of that night brought back memories for Bella and how she had been kidnapped all those years ago. Whatever Dankov and Mitch had between them, she knew it ran deep and that it was extremely dangerous.

They arrived at the narrow gates with high walls and barbed wire on top. They slowly passed through into the courtyard beyond.

As they walked into the building, they were shown to the briefing room.

"I could murder a cup of coffee," Mac stated, with somewhat a lack of sensitivity given their evening.

Bella understood and recognized the dark humor that she had become accustomed to from her own father.

Hotel d'Aubusson
Saint Germain des Prés, Paris, France
9:00 a.m.

Bella, Mitch, and Mac made it back to their hotel, had breakfast, and then went to their rooms to sleep off the night. The same Citroen bus had dropped them off. All three were exhausted from their nighttime exploits, both physically and mentally. It had been a busy few weeks with so much to comprehend, digest, and understand. It had all happened so quickly.

She got to her room of this beautiful Parisian boutique hotel in the heart of Paris's Saint Germain des Prés. Other times, she would have enjoyed the coffee shops, the restaurants, the shopping, and the bars, but this trip wasn't for fun. It was for necessity, and despite that, the taking of a human life, even if the enemy, was never a great cause for celebration, at least not for her. She didn't do the dark humor too well yet.

As she flopped on her bed, there was something that troubled her. Something was playing on her instincts. Or was it some sort of sixth sense?

Her eyes starting to close, she replayed the night in her mind. The team, the pause, the entry, the fierce action, being totally high on adrenaline, where minutes felt like seconds and vice versa as the scene before her slowed down like a frame-by-frame movie. She had first heard Mitch tell her about this phenomenon as a child, and she had witnessed the same as she became competent with the boxing gloves and competed at a high level.

She went through her thoughts, the ride, then the briefing, and then to the hotel.

In her mind, the frames slowed down further, which alerted her senses even more. Although they had arrived at nine in the morning, the playback revealed different faces at the concierge, a different face at reception, hints of an accent, not a Parisian accent though. It was not unusual in this cosmopolitan and diverse city, but then the replay didn't show any other guests. Although breakfast was brief, there was no one else in the dining room but the three of them.

She started to sit up slowly, very slowly, like some apparition was dawning upon her. She went over to her backpack and drew out the baton that she carried—not too long that it was wieldy, long enough that it nicely extended her reach, heavy enough to have brutal weight without making it slow, and innocent enough to get through any customs search.

As she pulled it out of the bag, there was a knock on the door. A rough man's voice, heavy accent. "Housekeeping."

Another double knock, harder this time.

"Housekeeping. Can we come in?"

Bella looked around her room and played out the scene before her. It was better for her to welcome them in than for them to storm the door, she decided. She looked at the bathroom door half-open, and that was her play.

"Oh yes, just a moment," she shouted. "I am just in the bathroom. Won't be a moment."

That was the cue for them to come in, and as she heard the electronic key activate the lock on her bedroom door, she slipped into the bathroom to give the would-be intruders a false sense of security.

She was relieved when she realized that there was just one of them. He was clearly over six feet tall and brandishing what looked like a P-96 in his hand. She was ready and prepared, and the movie was slowing down in her head. She was in the zone.

He started to inch open the door to the bathroom. She hoped to get him to go all the way inside. The small space would give her an advantage. The element of surprise then full, decisive and explosive force would be the combination that worked best.

Almost fully into the bathroom, it was Bella's time to strike. Baton to his hand, full force, broken bones, the gun dropped to the floor. Bella swung the baton, and with brutal force, she hit the left side of his head with a crushing blow, immediately followed by a backhand strike that made the same connection to his right temple and ear.

She wrapped the shower curtain over his head, and he fell to his knees. She bludgeoned him with the baton, carefully aimed strokes, crushing his nose with blood busting on the inside of the shower curtain. Two more to the right side of his temple. One at the weak point fulcrum of his jaw, likely breaking the joint. Then as he was on his knees, all but unconscious and in excruciating pain, the final coup de grâce to the back of his skull, full force, downward pressure, just like wielding the hammer at the fairground.

Ninety seconds from start to finish—surprise and full, brutal force.

The man was dead. She checked his pockets—Russian— then picked up his P-96 pistol, checked its magazine and load status, and headed to find Mitch.

She knew where his room was, the far right, top balcony of the seventeenth-century façade of d'Aubusson, above the Café Laurent. Rather than taking the obvious route one, sticking to her plan of surprise, she scaled the canopy above the café to the first-floor windowsills of the guest rooms above. Grabbing the iron railing of the top floor, she pulled herself up and into the shallow balcony of Mitch's room.

Mitch was tied up to one of the Louis XV reproduction chairs, heavy and beautiful, along with the other furnishings of the d'Aubusson that she had admired.

"What a waste of a beautiful chair," she whispered to herself. "Problem with Russians is that they simply have no fucking taste."

Bella peered through the patio doors and the net curtains inside. Mitch was covered in blood, looking in bad shape as the bigger of the two was punching him, the brass knuckle duster doing its work.

She could have broken the flimsy lock on the doors, but there was no need, as they were carelessly not locked and just pulled to.

Bella paused for a moment and played the scene out in her mind. Bursting through the doors, keeping her footing, double tap number one, double tap number two. Headshots. Immediate result.

Keeping her balance and landing on her feet, giving her enough time to get her shots off was the biggest risk here, of many.

Without giving them the advantage of advanced notice of her arrival, she swung on the wrought iron, gathered all of her weight and speed, and crashed into the double doors with her feet kicking the middle of the partially engaged lock and bursting the doors open.

The big man with the knuckle dusters, surprised, looked at the doors. *Pop, pop.* Down. Dead. Perfect shots exploding the back of his head against the wall.

Number two had moved and was more agile than she had assumed, jumping to her left side, grabbing her shoulder and ripping the P-96 from her grip, spinning it on the floor toward the bathroom and away from both Mitch and Bella.

For a moment, the second Russian was gaining advantage. Bella grabbed the baton from her waistband and shoved it right into the Russian's left eye, with full force and deliberate intent to remove the eye from its socket. Not quite sharp enough to achieve her goal, the baton did penetrate the skull and give the recipient enough pain for her to take back the advantage. Although a big bear of a man, he was in pain. She brought round the baton and with full force connected with his jaw. She didn't have enough leverage and speed to make the most impact, but it was sufficient to add more pain to her target.

She had a chance to stand up, which made the odds swing in her favor, and as he tried to stand up, she kicked him in the side of his head, by his temple, also trying to take advantage of the positive benefits of the left ear. A second blow with the baton crashed in that perfect spot, with the Russian responding with a wince and a scream.

She scrambled for the P-96 and took two shots to the back of the head, blood and brains bursting around the room, onto the marble floor. Dead.

At that moment, the front door to Mitch's room burst open, and in came crashing Mac, looking around at Mitch tied up, the two dead bodies, and Bella.

"How come you started the party without me?"

Breaking News: CRN News Network News: Russian Peacekeeping Force Enters Equatorial Guinea

"Reporting from Malabo, Equatorial Guinea, this is Josh Penbury from CRN New Network reporting to you live.

"Well, we had a few hours of intense fighting between the rebels and government forces. There were several explosions that lit up the night sky, but it seemed obvious that the EG security forces were no match in terms of equipment or training.

"No one seems to know where the rebels came from, but observers say that number one, they are not African. They are mostly white skinned. And number two, despite their American vehicles, they are certainly not speaking American, whatever that means.

"Then about thirty minutes ago, in rolled the first of what has been identified as a Russian peacekeeping vehicle, bringing troops into the city, setting up what seem like security posts around the city. The military vehicles, armor, and tanks are all painted white with the Russian flag flaring and *миротворчество, mirotvorchestvo* or *peacekeepers*.

"Malabo has gone through a flash pan and escalation of violence back to relative calm in just a matter of days and is now back to normal, apart from blazing cars and fires as they continue to smolder, with the Russian peacekeepers on every corner.

"There appears little sign of the rebels and certainly no resistance with the Russian forces, as they retreated peacefully to a compound just outside the city center.

"This is Josh Penbury reporting, CRN News, Malabo."

BGPC Compound
Malabo, Equatorial Guinea, West Africa
6:00 a.m.

It was still dark in Malabo as the cavalcade made its way through the streets, burning cars and buildings, creating havoc but not one that looked like a coup, maybe more a mini revolution. The damage was minimal, and that pleased the occupants of the black SUVs dashing through the city to their rendezvous point, the compound and headquarters of the British Gas & Pipeline Corporation on the edge of the city.

As they approached the compound, about a quarter of a mile away, they could spot the collection of armaments and vehicles that they had funded and those of the rebel force too, tightly and safely retreated to this enclave and fortress they had created.

In a straight line, one after another, they weren't expecting hostilities. They were, after all, the creators, the funders, the architects. They were the Presidential Six.

Sitting underground at the heart of the complex were the remote monitors and controls for the mounted .50-caliber machine guns. Just like in a video game, the controllers would be devoid of any intimate contact, just through the extension of the deadly weapons.

Despite the armor plating of the six SUVs and best intentions of their creators, they were no match for the .50-caliber Brownings that started to let loose.

The first hit the driver of the first vehicle in the head, making it explode like a pumpkin at a showground fair. Then the full force of the three machine guns let rip. The vehicles stopped dead in their tracks, the occupants within stunned.

The rebel force then, in a reaction, focused a dozen RPG-32s at the cavalcade and within milliseconds destroyed it and the occupants in their ill-fitting Savile Row suits and misguided ambitions of power.

Dobroy nochi. Good night. With love from Moscow.

Breaking News: CRN News Network: Equatorial Guinea under Rebel Control

"Reporting from Malabo, Equatorial Guinea, this is Josh Penbury from CRN News Network reporting to you live.

"Malabo has been quiet now for a couple of hours. We have seen several incidents of the Presidential Guard surrendering to the still unknown force, and just moments ago, we saw one of the rebel's vehicles going through the gates with what could have been Celestino Romada Racale entering the palace as president.

"The scenes are incredible as the crowded streets have turned from protests and violence into scenes of jubilation with chants for their new president and newfound freedom.

"It seems that there is plenty of reason to celebrate tonight in Malabo and thank the Russian peacekeeping force for helping them.

"We can see people with placards and pictures of Racale with our president, and then in the crowds, there are placards with images of Putin, *Our Savior*.

"This is truly extraordinary.

"This is Josh Penbury reporting, CRN News, Malabo."

PART V

FLIP SIDE

23
HOUSE AT THE BACK

10 Downing Street
City of Westminster, London
8:00 a.m.

DIGBY STROLLED UP TO THE black door of No. 10 about fifteen minutes after both the foreign secretary and the home secretary arrived in their Jaguar XJ50s, black, cream leather, armor-plated. He paused to announce himself to the token bobby at the door and waited for the door to open before him, regretting not having the chance to use the big brass door knocker to mark his entrance.

He strolled inside and was met by a young lady, five foot four, petite, dark brown hair, deep brown eyes, and dressed as he would expect a prime minister's private secretary to be—black suit, pencil skirt, sensible shoes with a slight lift, and starched white shirt with a spread collar, almost resembling the look of a barrister. It was a look that Digby often admired, although he enjoyed the pinstripe version more.

Sarah took him into the depths of the famous Georgian townhouse built in the 1680s by George Downing, a notorious spy for Oliver Cromwell then later Charles I. Digby had done his homework. He liked the detail. He liked to know not only the what but the why. He found that depth of knowledge helped him in his job. The why was always important and not less so than the events over the past few days.

It was a true honor to be invited to No. 10, and Digby thought it was a true indication of his career path progression after his time with the Blues and Royals.

Either that, or he had a steal on other intelligence agencies, and the intel bought to him by Beecham earlier that month had given him a step up.

In this instance, although a marriage of unlikely bed partners, the *why* was a convergence of very logical business reasons. One: the Russians were relishing their return to influence and world power play. Two: the Mexican cartels had in effect called a truce with one another to focus on business. Three: this fit in with the Russian agenda of destabilizing democracy and especially undermining the US. And four: they would all make a lot of money doing it.

Power and greed. A common theme since the beginning of mankind, Digby thought. *Power, greed, and money.*

The whole notion of a sovereign state using criminal tactics to achieve its aims. Of a criminal cartel turning to traditional business as a means, the cooperation of the remaining cartels, destabilizing the election of a small but oil-rich nation, the rebel force, the coincidental proximity of the Russian peacekeeping force and ultimately the takeover of the sixth-largest oil-producing nation in Africa, producing three hundred thousand barrels today but with reported reserves to potentially make it number one in the Africa rankings.

"Genius. Pure fucking genius," Digby had repeatedly said to himself over the past week or so.

And as he thought about the potential reaction from the West, well, what could they do? On the international stage, Russia appeared to be exerting its resources to stabilize an unstable situation, uphold peace, restore democracy, remove a greedy dictator, and restore faith in the people.

"Fucking genius."

He followed Sarah around the corridors that felt like a warren, just like the master spy Downing, who built this residence, had intended. *It adds to the experience of being here*, thought Digby with a smile.

Sarah stopped at a large double door and politely knocked. "Enter" came from the other side. Sarah stepped aside, opening the door and ushering Digby in with her other hand. Digby stepped through to the briefing room, with just six of the twenty-two spaces taken. Digby was the seventh and final attendee for this meeting.

The plasma screens on the back wall were playing the latest footage of the protestors-turned-campaigners walking around Malabo with placards celebrating their savior, Vladimir Putin, and the Russian liberators. There were as many of the Equatorial Guinea green, white, and red flags as the red, white, and blue Russian flag, and many were celebrating with both. According to sources on the ground, there were folks giving away the flags to the crowd for free. Typical Kremlin propaganda.

The commentary praised the support of Russia, avoiding yet another bloody civil war in Africa. Putin would visit Racale in the next few days to consummate what would be a historic day in Africa, with speculation that Russia might have its first official colony in Africa since Sagallo in the late 1880s. Yes, it was true that they had had eyes on the continent for some time, including supporting the Central African Republic fight the marauding militias and supporting the regime in South Yemen, but this was different. This was much different.

"What can the Western world do apart from join in the applause?" asked the prime minister to her small audience. Beyond diplomacy, what else could they do? The Russians had played it well, and it would be hard for any other nation to criticize them on the global stage.

"Did you know in Russia, Putin has made a public joke of how they get blamed for everything? If we criticize them for preventing civil war and potential genocide, then the joke will quickly turn on us."

The small audience looked at their pads on the antique mahogany meeting table, leaving the foreign secretary to fill the silence. "Well, Prime Minister, I think the long and short of it is that there isn't much we can do."

The home secretary added, "Maybe joining in the congratulations might be the smartest diplomatic move."

The prime minister nodded. "Yes, Mr. Home Secretary, perhaps you are right. Checkmate. Good game." She looked at the monitors, flicked a switch, and the room was silent.

"Time to get on with our own crisis here at home," she announced.

Hacienda de San Pedro Mártir
Coyoacán, Mexico City, Mexico
6:30 a.m.

Bianca Blanca woke up to the morning sunshine and the sound of the birds making their morning chorus and getting ready for their day. She felt the familiar and comforting Egyptian linen sheets and saw the shimmer of morning sunshine on the carved ceiling beams above her. She checked the time, six thirty, and rolled over to see Paulo Mancini's eyes flickering in the morning sunshine as he came out of a deep and comforting sleep. She reached over and touched his muscular and olive-skinned chest and went further down to say good morning, followed by kisses to his belly button and below. When he was ready, she scooted on top, and they both writhed together like a pair of ballet dancers, enjoying their bodies and enjoying this intimate moment together until satisfaction.

The Hacienda de San Pedro Mártir, situated in a quiet neighborhood of Mexico City, was Bianca's main home. The walled property had expansive gardens and courtyards, cellars, a secret corner, and its own chapel. The red plaster façade and the paved walkways around the grounds made an oasis in this hustle-and-bustle city, away from her stressful and dangerous day job.

She walked to the balcony of the master bedroom, naked, tall, slender, athletic but muscular, her long blonde hair down the smooth contours of her back, like the mane of a rare and exotic panther.

Bianca looked at the gardens below her and smiled to herself. The last few years had been worth it. The last few weeks, the plan had come to a climax. She looked over at Paulo getting dressed and smiled again, thinking of where she came from all those years ago, how far she had come today.

This was the closest to satisfaction she had ever encountered, but she knew that the danger had not gone away and likely never would. That created a sadness in her that she would never again venture down to the flower market again, or pop into her favorite restaurant for breakfast, go to the ballet that she so loved—not without her very large and growing security detail.

She was a Mexican icon, a celebrity of sorts, and probably the most powerful woman in Mexico, if not Latin America, perhaps even the world, she surmised. These were accolades that she had aspired to, that filled her with pride and her various bank accounts with money, but she had discovered that true happiness wasn't just about money.

As Paulo approached from behind her and wrapped his arms around her waist, she realized that it was too late in the day to turn back. There was nowhere to turn. That would be too dangerous and ultimately result in her assassination by one of the many enemies she had made over the years, or just someone who wanted to claim her crown for themselves.

Mancini and Blanca had been lovers over the years, but their relationship was growing closer. They were both independent, smart thinkers. Beneath the business, they were both involved; they had big ambitions but good intentions. They admired each other, they fueled each other, they spurred each other on—not by long conversations over dinner, or mentoring each other through complex plans. In fact, it was the opposite: in silence. In their business, you don't share plans. They are strictly preserved for your own mind, just like a classical composer would arrange the symphony and the orchestra in their head. That was exactly how Blanca went through her business.

Any kind of indiscretion could get you killed in Mexico, especially in her line of business. Her relationship with Mancini was more like a collision of strength that refueled the body and the mind, a feeling that they both had, as evidenced by the fact they were spending more and more time together when they could.

They both knew this. They didn't need to talk about it. Gesture and deed were good enough for both of them.

Mancini draped a diamond-encrusted holy cross necklace around Blanca's neck and fastened it behind as the cross nestled atop her cleavage between her perfectly formed breasts.

"A present from your Colombian friend," he whispered in her ear. "These are the finest diamonds, the cross of Jesus, and the love from my heart. This is my present to you, Bianca Blanca."

Bianca looked down and scooped up the cross to look at the beautiful, sparkling gift. *What do you buy a woman who has everything?* she asked herself. *Answer: something from the heart.*

She turned in his arms, looked in his eyes, and kissed him on the lips. "Paulo, you are a beautiful man."

"Bianca, you are the most beautiful woman in the world."

"We're now in not just the retail business but the global retail business." She smiled with pride.

"And the oil business," he countered.

"Let's go for breakfast and pop a cork." She winked, he agreed, and they headed to the secret garden in the grounds of the Hacienda de San Pedro Mártir.

24
FAREWELL

British Gas & Pipeline
Corporation Headquarters
Malabo, Equatorial Guinea, West Africa
12:55 a.m.

BOB HAD SEEN THE FIREWORKS kick off from his hotel room at the Hilton earlier that night, the flashes and bangs in the east as the airport was being taken. He could see and hear the various skirmishes in the city as the rebel force neared the Government Building. He could also hear the various assault vehicles some with their high-pitched whine and others with their deep, rumbling groans as they entered and progressed through the city.

Bob guessed that the uptick in flashes, bangs, and violence just a few blocks away was the heightened resistance from the Presidential Guard as the palace was targeted as the final part of this lightning invasion.

The Equatorial troops were simply not up to any credible threat from a professional force, and that was confirmed by the speed with which this force was making progress. Bob decided to head down to the BGPC headquarters, and as he got to the front of the Hilton, he commandeered a BMW R1200 motorcycle parked outside, much to the valet's protests.

After all, they were in the midst of a revolution, he thought.

As Bob left the Hilton behind him and made his way through the deserted streets of Malabo, he saw the flashes, heard the bangs, and smelled the familiar aroma of battle in the air. He breathed in, remembering ventures past.

As he made his way to the compound, he passed the convoy of limos, a bullet-riddled, burnt-out, crumpled mess. He guessed the demise of the Presidential Six and grunted as he slowed briefly and then sped past.

Bob arrived at the gate under the gaze of the watchtowers and the .50-caliber M2s. With no helmet, he was recognized by the security guards as he made his way into the compound and the new headquarters building.

Hamza Malik was waiting for him.

"Well, well, well, the prodigal son returns again," said Malik, with his familiar hiss and hostility. Bob was still trying to work out the genesis of the undertone. He only knew Malik as a Legionnaire, that he came from Algerian decent, was orphaned in his teens, and went off to the French Foreign Legion as a means of escape.

"Did you get the news?" Bob asked, ignoring the tone. He could tell by Malik's reaction that he had not.

"Your sister and the kids are safe," he stated. "In a safe house just outside of Paris."

Malik looked up at Bob and acknowledged the news with a nod.

"My fucking pleasure, Hamza! Now what the fuck is going on with you?"

Hamza Malik took Bob inside to one of the briefing rooms and explained the full story about how the Presidential Six had approached him and used the past to haunt him. "Yes, your past, Bob. While you were sunning yourself on some sunny beach, I was picking up the tab for you." He looked at Bob with anger.

Bob just looked at him, allowing Malik to vent.

"Where were you, Bob? Where the fuck was Big Bad Bob when I needed him?"

Bob shrugged. "How the fuck was I to know, Hamza?"

"Says the man who knows fucking everything," Malik countered. "I'm in too deep, Bob. I know too much. I cannot cross back."

Bob looked at him, trying to work out what he meant by that, thinking through potential eventualities here, surrounded by a Russian peacekeeping force of sorts, remembering his panic password from his design of the building. The magic word would instantly shut off all systems, lock the doors, and effect his escape, if he needed it.

It was Bob's secret addition to the security design. Only the installation contractor knew of it. He hoped it hadn't got out. He hoped it hadn't changed.

Malik mused, "They will be here soon, in their new home." He looked around him and went to his waist to pull out his pistol.

Bob shouted, "Bollocks!" The lights went off immediately. Bob slid to the side in the darkness, hearing and seeing the two rounds going off, past his head and into the wall behind him. Swinging deep left, he leveled his left hook at Malik's temple and with the other grabbed Malik's pistol hand. He bent Malik's hand backward, dropping the weapon on the ground as they fell together.

The much bigger and much more experienced Bob wrestled his way around Malik so that he was behind Malik, on the floor. He put Malik's neck into the crease of his right elbow, grabbed his own wrist, and like a guillotine, pulled and squeezed, blocking the blood flow to Malik's brain. Within a few moments, he felt Malik go to sleep. At least for a while. Bob would tie him up, gag him, and leave him to his newfound friends. He wasn't inclined to finish him off as his instincts and training were telling him to.

Outside, he could hear the rumble of vehicles entering the compound. "They're here already. Farewell, my friend." He looked down at Malik and went into the labyrinth of the offices, making his way to the underground bunker and the secret exit tunnel he'd had built.

Thankfully for Bob, no one knew this building like he did. After all, he did design it.

He found the exit hatch, opened the door, and dropped down the chute into the underground tunnel. He jumped into one of the Dragonfire Racing Polaris ATVs, fired up the engine, and sped off into the dark of the tunnel, away from the rebel force occupying the compound behind him.

In his time in Equatorial Guinea, he had long realized the need for having at least one escape option. He would be a very unwelcome guest of Boris Latminko and his new sidekick, Hamza Malik.

The first time he had ever met Malik, when he went to Malabo to apparently take Bob out, he recognized a sense of weakness, a sense of naivete and desperation. Bob had felt sorry for him and helped him, perhaps blinded by his own desire to leave this shithole. As he drove through the dark, he beat himself up for what could have been a deadly mistake.

He headed straight, top speed, feeling the need once again to get out of this shithole and never return.

He exited the tunnel into the cool, early-morning Malabo air, then headed down to the waterfront to the marina and one of his other escape mechanisms, his boat, *Dignity*.

He ditched the ATV in the harbor, making sure it sank in water deep enough to hide it from plain view. Then he hurried down the floating dock to the T at the end. His magnificent yacht was tied up there, ready to go at a moment's notice. He jumped aboard his ride, a 101-foot performance cruiser designed by Nauta. With four bedrooms, two salons, one mast, and twin sails, it was a beautifully understated yacht with a dark blue hull and wooden decking, all funded courtesy of the British Gas & Pipeline Corporation, registered in his fictitious name, Maynard Keynes. A forward investment proving its worth tonight.

He'd fully planned for a quick escape and to be able to disappear for a good long while. He had plenty of food. The yacht was equipped with a water maker, and she had plenty of tankage as well. The extra fuel would help the twin sails. His favorite store of composite rations would tide him over at least for a couple of months. As he hurried to the bridge to fire up the big twin diesels to warm them up, he was pleased that he had a stash of his favorite Liddlesdale whisky on board. He would be fine. In fact, he would be more than fine.

Bob left the bridge, cast off the lines, and guided the yacht out of the harbor. She'd be a bit tricky to handle solo, but he was quite capable. He had the skills to safely cruise the three thousand nautical miles around the ear of Africa and on to Gran Canaria. When he was safely offshore, he set the autopilot. The lights of Malabo disappeared behind him to the south. He pulled a bottle of the Liddlesdale, a pack of cigars, put his feet up, and thought through the events of the day.

He turned on the stereo, his favorite track, "Deacon Blue, Dignity."

He looked at the open ocean in front of him and the bottle of whisky. He took another draw of his cigar, boomed a big smile, and thought of his journey home and his permanent retirement.

"I'm too old for this shit," he grunted as the next of his favorite tracks started.

25
KEEP YOUR ENEMIES CLOSE

The Paris Ritz
15 Place Vendome, Paris, France
4:00 p.m.

BELLA AND MITCH ARRIVED AT the Ritz and made their way to the Salon Proust to meet their appointment that afternoon. *A civilized afternoon tea and a public place—what better way to meet with a deep, dark enemy and avoid any unpleasantries*, Bella thought.

They had heard on good authority from Chip, Beecham, and Digby that Dankov was in Paris. They also knew that Dankov knew that Mitch was in Paris, following the news of his operatives being dispatched. Digby and his connection to the Kremlin had managed to broker a face-to-face meeting between the two.

Mitch had been ranting all the way to the Ritz. He had read his copy of the *London Times* that morning and seen that Martin McGuiness had been awarded a Certificate of

Honor by the city of San Francisco. Its description quoted "courageous military service" as one of the reasons. He was still chuntering as they walked into the Ritz. Bella politely listened; she knew it was a subject that she best not get involved in, although she had her own opinions about the former IRA man and his exploits.

They took their seats in the Grand Salon. Bella watched the man behind the baby grand piano cranking out old Parisian favorites with his gravelly voice, his adept fingers caressing the ivory keyboard of the vintage piano.

The occupants of this afternoon's high tea were among the wealthiest of Paris or visiting tourists who were able to afford the riches of this Grande Dame in its center.

They chose this venue as a place of relative safety, a public place, while also for the privacy of this exclusive establishment full of its traditions, its airs, its graces, and its discretion.

At exactly 4:20 p.m. and fashionably late, Dankov strode into the room, his big frame imposing itself upon the room with the presence of a man who would stop at nothing to meet his ends. Bella knew this of him. She loathed him, despised him, and hated him as much if not more than her father did.

Dankov strode over to the two with no signs of any impediments as a result from his prosthetic leg. The only visible signs were the scars from the severe burns down the right side of his face, where the melted skin had once dripped.

Mitch and Bella politely stood up. Dankov waved his hands. "Please, please, sit down," he said as he joined them.

There was an awkward silence until the waiter arrived, and they placed their order for high tea for three. When the waiter left, they began to talk business.

"Very civilized," Bella said, the sarcasm in her voice louder than her choice of words.

Dankov looked at her with a smile but with the eyes of a rabid dog about to eat his prey, knowing his master would not approve.

He looked at Mitch. "Fine young lady, Mitchell. She grows up, yes?"

"What? Since you last kidnapped her, Dmitri?" Mitch shot back with an equally sarcastic smile.

"Now, now, Mitchell. That is history. We are not here to go over that old ground but establish new. No? Give us this daily bread to forgive our trespasses, as we forgive trespasses against us." He smiled.

"That's the fucking Lord's Prayer," snapped Mitch.

"Or close to it," said Bella.

"Mitchell, Mitchell, Mitchell." Dankov stroked the right side of his face. "You forgive me for my indiscretions, and I might forgive you for trying to blow me the fuck up. How's that for compromise?"

"You know that wasn't me. You already took care of that with Yee. I was there just to witness the pain in the same way that you have inflicted pain on me and my family."

"Mitchell, like me, you are a warrior, you are a soldier for your nation. We are adversaries in conflict, but the war is over, my friend." He looked into Mitch's soul. "It is not good for either of us to continue this. It must be over between us. Mitchell, it's bad for business and for our health. No?"

"Well, Dmitri, you call off your hounds, and I will stop putting them down," Mitch said.

The three different flavors of tea arrived, an English Breakfast for Mitch, an Earl Grey for Bella, and a Kusmi Russian tea for Dankov.

After the tea was poured and the waiter left their table, Dankov said, "You know, Mitchell, you can tell a lot of a person from what tea they drink."

All three took a sip of their tea and admired the four-level stack of finger sandwiches and cakes before them, although in present company, Bella wasn't hungry. She noticed that Mitchel and Dankov didn't grab a sandwich either. They all just sat there with their tea, eyeing one another like caged lions.

"Today, I propose that we call truce. Today, I propose that we let the past be and allow each other to get on with our own business. Yours with yours and mine with mine."

Bella leaned forward over the edge of the table as she focused intently on what Dankov was saying. She wondered if it was possible to call off the violence, or whether this was just another one on Dankov's dirty tricks.

"How can I be sure this isn't a trick?" Mitch asked, mirroring her exact thoughts.

"You can be sure. You have friends in important places in this world, my friend." Mitch looked at Dankov and to Bella.

"Our new business partner, Bianca Blanca, made this request."

Bella was confused, and she could see that Mitch was too.

"She made the request on behalf of an old friend of yours and a new and influential friend of ours, Mr. Paulo Mancini."

Dankov smiled. Bella got the sense that he was enjoying their apparent confusion. "You see, we are making big changes. We're pretty much out of the drug trade, or we will be soon. Bianca has arranged a truce among the cartels."

Bella raised an eyebrow. "A truce? Yeah, sure. Like that's really going to happen."

Dankov sipped his tea. "It already has happened. And we want it to happen between us and you as well. So, what do you say, Mitch?"

Bella could see that her dad felt conflicted. She did too. In a way, the conflict gave them purpose, something to fight for and against. Having that gone might leave a hole in their lives.

"Dankov, you have my word. You stay away from me and mine, and I will stay away from you. Okay?"

"Yes, yes, yes. It is a deal. You have my word. As of this day, we are friends, no?" Dankov held out his hand as he stood up. Mitch accepted, as did Bella, and Dankov walked back out the way that he came.

70 Beach Road
Harrogate, North Yorkshire, United Kingdom
7:45 a.m.

Sara jumped into her Golf GTI and headed across town to Bob's apartment on Beach Road. She had done this several times over the past few weeks, just checking in to see if there were any signs of life.

She hadn't seen or heard anything from Bob since that night in the Ivy, when he had popped the question. His mobile phone went straight to voice mail. No response from her emails or texts, and his team at Grace & Co had not heard from him either. Just when she thought she had found the right man to settle down with, he went AWOL. As the days turned into weeks, and the weeks to months, she was losing hope. Sara knew that this was a big commitment for Bob, a departure, a new chapter, a level of trepidation maybe, but that didn't help her as she was lost in limbo, not knowing the answer when her friends asked her.

Through the windows, the apartment looked exactly as he had left it; nothing changed apart from the amount of mail growing daily.

She had asked around—Alan, John Paul, Claire—if they had heard from him, and the same answer came, "Not a dickey bird."

She was worried. At first, she thought he might have gotten cold feet, but as the weeks went by, she was concerned for his well-being.

"Where the fuck are you, Bob?" she said as she looked through the letter box before jumping back in the Golf and heading to work.

Dignity
Atlantic Ocean
Off the Coast of West Africa

Bob was an accomplished sailor. As a boy, he had enjoyed visiting the Lake District with his father and taking their sail boat, the *DawnE,* around Windermere in all seasons, summer, winter, rain or shine. It was his time with his father.

Just Bob and him. Sailing, fishing, listening to old tales, swimming, hunting, getting to know each other. Probably the happiest days of his life until his father died when Bob was only fifteen. He joined the army shortly after.

Bob purchased *Dignity* while working for BGPC as a double backup, an exit plan if he ever needed it, and his advance planning and preparation had paid off. He always knew that exiting over land was the most treacherous option and with the most likelihood of getting caught, fleeing whatever danger might exist. The airport was small, and passing though unobserved wasn't a possibility, even with a fake passport. Everyone knew everyone in Malabo, especially Bob. Everyone knew Big Bad Bob.

He had left the port of Malabo in the dead of night, sailed past the Bight of Biafra Bay by midmorning next day, and then that night past the Gulf of Guinea, skirting round the ear of Africa up the west coast. He had decided not to hit land until he got to the Canaries, where he would pull into Las Palmas and see a few friends he had there—world travelers, a mix of interesting characters and stories to tell. He was enjoying his own company as he cruised northward under full sail. He always liked his alone time. For the most part, like many of his kind, he preferred that to the company of others.

He had made contact with Lord Beecham and arranged to meet him and their friend Penny for dinner and a catch-up. He told Beecham that his whereabouts were on a need-to-know basis and just between the two of them.

"Loose lips sink ships, old boy" was the rather predictable response from the somewhat eccentric but intensely loyal and resourceful Beecham. He was a very handy man to know and have on his side when in a tight spot.

He would stay for a couple or so days, get *Dignity* moored up in her new home, the Rubicon Marina, and head out from there, wherever he might go next. Returning to Harrogate was one option.

The Union Club
Greek Street, London, United Kingdom
12:30 p.m.

The Union Bar was quiet, as always, and that was just the way Bella liked it. There had been too much going on of late. She smiled at Collins and her dad, popped a chip into her mouth, and said, "Well, what's next, Dad?"

They had two fish 'n' chips and a steak sandwich between them. Two Old Speckled Hens and a glass of Californian Macrostie Chardonnay. The three friends went over the events of the past few weeks, discussing what was next, when and how it would all play out.

Bella said, "This is kinda worrying if the same tactics are applied to other vulnerable countries. What about what's happening in other parts of Africa?"

"And in Venezuela and Cuba," added Collins.

"Burma," said Mitch.

They tucked into their casual lunch. Proper fish 'n' chips was one of the things that she and Mitch missed about the UK. Not much was said until they finished eating. Mitch dabbed his mouth with his napkin, put the napkin down, and said, "That hit the spot."

Bella laughed. "How could it not hit the spot?"

Collins took a sip of his drink and asked about the Dankov meeting. "I really didn't see that one coming," he said. "Why do you suppose he wants to stop trying to take you out?"

Mitch stroked his chin, looking pensive. Bella had seen that look on his face a lot lately. "I really can't say. I figure maybe he thinks it's better to not have me on his case."

"Well, he'd be right about that," Bella said, feeling pride in her father and his lethal abilities. "Besides, he says Paulo Mancini lobbied for a peace treaty. Guess there was pressure coming from more than one side."

"I suppose that's true," Collins said. "In any case, it's good news for all of us. If he could take Yee out, then he definitely could pose an ongoing danger to us."

"Yeah, I can sleep easier not having to look over my shoulder all the time," Mitch said. "Not that I don't anyway. Look over my shoulder, I mean."

"We know what you mean, Dad."

Collins ordered two more the Old Speckled Hens, Mitch's favorite beer from the Morland Brewery up the road in Suffolk.

Mac came in the front door and joined them, ordering a third Speckled Hen. He had been wrapping things up with the real estate agents. Houses like his didn't come up too often. It had sold—job done, cash buyer, big smile on his face. Villa Valparaiso was one step closer.

"You'll never guess who I just bumped into!" Mac said.

"Who? Were they fucking Russian? Equatorial Guineans?" asked Mitch.

"Animal, vegetable, or mineral?" teased Collins.

"Or maybe Mexicans?" chimed in Bella between sips of MacRostie.

"You'd never guess who it was," Mac said.

"So then bloody well tell us, Mac," Collins said.

"Jose fucking Mourinho."

"Who? The former Manchester United boss?" Collins asked.

"The very same."

"You mean the one that just announced today he is going to host a fucking football TV show on Russian TV?" asked Mitch.

"Are you fucking serious?" Mac asked.

"Saw it on the news this morning," Mitch said.

The table found that highly amusing.

"What complex lives you all lead, boys," Bella said with a smile. She winked at Mitch and the other two men at the table.

The conversation went on about Sam and the loss of Emily, the loss of Jimmy, and Bella's recent visit to Bangkok to see his widow, Jenni.

"How is Jenni?" asked Mac.

"Seems to be doing fine. The Oasis still looks like it's doing well. She's hooked up with some sailor from Maine. Seemed happy enough."

"That didn't take her long," Collins said.

"Well, you just gotta move on," Mitch replied.

"No point in hanging around. Life's too short," Mac said.

Another round of laughter was followed by another round of drinks.

"Has anyone heard from Bob?" Mitch asked the group.

"Bob? Where the fuck is Bob?" Mac piped in, and they all broke into laughter again.

Meson El Maño
Las Palmas, Gran Canaria
Canary Islands
10:30 a.m.

Lord Beecham had spotted *Dignity* sailing elegantly into Las Palmas. He was eating breakfast when he received a call on the satellite phone he always kept nearby, just in case one of his operatives needed to reach him in a hurry. He answered the call and was delighted to hear Bob's voice.

"Hello, my old boy!" Beecham said. "Where you at?"

Bob greeted him warmly and said he was closing in on the outer harbor.

"Okay, great!" Beecham said. "I'll meet you at the marina in about an hour."

He ended the call, pleased about the safe passage of his friend out of harm's way, to a new life that hopefully would contain more peace than violence. He finished his breakfast and then headed to the Rubicon Marina, a facility that Beecham had recommended. His friend Penny had lived there for several years, or at least she had a base there while galivanting around the world on her various expeditions.

She had worked with Beecham for twenty-plus years, longer than Beecham cared to remember.

As Beecham watched Bob's boat glide into the harbor, he admired the beauty of what he guessed could be a Perini

Navi production, based on its elegant styling, dark blue hull, and finely crafted planks.

"Very fine boat, old boy," he said in admiration.

Beecham had a love of the sea and a love of super yachts, and although *Dignity* may not have quite fallen into that category, it was a mighty fine example.

As a young man, his father, a Royal Navy man, managed to get Beecham a ride with the Royal Naval Sailing team, and in turn, that got Beecham onto a luxury charter as chief engineer, and he spent the next four years sailing the world. Indeed, that was where he first met Penny, the ship's chef. Penny had made the first introductions to one of the guests, now Beecham's wife.

As per the arrangements he'd made with Bob when he called on the satellite phone, Beecham made his way to one of his favorite little places, Meson El Maño, which overlooked the marina. When Bob finished squaring away the yacht, he would join Beecham for a long lunch. Beecham glanced at the bottle of Dom Perignon on ice and the plate of fat steamed oysters on the half shell. He looked forward to welcoming Bob back to civilization.

26
STARMAN

Four Months Later
The Old Station Inn
Birstwith, North Yorkshire, United Kingdom
3:30 p.m.

MITCH COULDN'T HELP BUT NOTICE how nervous Bob seemed as he nursed a stiff whisky at the Old Station Inn, one the group's favorite watering holes. "Calm down, Bob," Mitch said, hoisting his pint. "It's only a wedding."

"Yeah, but it's his wedding," Mac said.

"A joyous affair if there ever was one," Sam said.

Mitch noted the sadness in the eyes of his old friend. The loss of his wife, Emily, weighed heavily on him, and it probably always would. Time healed all, but time couldn't fill the void left behind.

"Indeed," Mitch said.

He was glad they'd all gotten together for prewedding calm-me-downs before heading to Ripley Castle for the main event. Soon it was time to go, and Mitch paid the tab. "Come on, Bob," he said. "It's time to meet your maker."

"Very funny," Bob said as they all left the bar and made their way to Mac's smart-looking Audi A8.

"Nice car, Mac," Sam said.

"Did you win the fucking lottery?" Bob asked.

"No, mate, I managed to syphon off some oil from the BGPC pipeline as their head of security was asleep at the wheel," Mac said.

Mac unlocked the car, and they all got in.

"I wasn't asleep at any wheel," Bob said.

Mac started the engine and put the car in drive as they began the short ride from Birstwith to Ripley. Within ten minutes, they had arrived in Ripley, where they parked outside the Boars Head. They walked over the cobbles down toward the main entrance of the castle, through the castle gates, and into the gravel-covered courtyard to the front of the castle overlooking the lake before it.

"Wow, Bob, this is fancy," Sam said.

"Just our local castle," Bob replied.

"Well if you're gonna take the plunge," Mac said.

"Anyone can slum it, Mac. It takes class to do it in style," Bob said.

As they headed to the wedding ceremony, Mitch laughed at the old humor, recalling days gone by, sleeping out in whatever environment they found themselves—desert, the tundra, forests, or fields and the reference to old soldiers' luxuries that were accumulated over time. Bob's favorite had been the canvass cot that raised just a few inches off the ground, giving an extra layer of comfort and saving them from the excruciating experience of sleeping on the ground.

"You're all class and style, Bob. Class and style." Sam slapped him on the back.

"Wait for the fireworks later, my friends," Bob said. "Hey, there's my new crew!" Bob said, beaming. He waved them over and introduced them to Mitch and the others as they headed into the castle and the civil ceremony room to the left of the grand entrance.

"Are you ready?" asked Mac.

"As I'll ever be," Bob said.

"Greatest day of your life," reassured Sam.

"Besides, you should be grateful you found someone, you old bugger," said Mac.

"I try before I buy." Bob laughed, slapping Mac on the back a bit harder than normal.

They walked in together. The grand entrance was wood paneled, with oil paintings surrounding them and looking down upon them, the approving or disapproving of the Ingleby ancestry making their judgments. Across the wooden floor, at the end, in the formal room were rows of twenty chairs in front of a table, and then three chairs, one for the minister and one each for the bride and groom.

The string quartet and the piano playing Pachelbel's Canon in G completed the scene overlooking the lake. Polite silence, smiles, and nods of encouragement came from the audience. Bob and Sam took their places at the front of the congregation, and after a short wait, the music switched to Handel's *Arrival of the Queen of Sheba*.

In a rare instance of emotion, he reached down and grabbed Sam's hand and squeezed. Just for a second. He had been at Sam and Emily's wedding all those years ago, and he could feel Sam's pain as they waited for Bob's bride-to-be, Sara.

The Palmilla Resort
San Jose del Cabo, Baja California, Mexico
6:00 p.m.

Bella and Mitch arrived at the beautiful, ornate gates of the Palmilla. They went up the paved driveway to the plain white chapel on the hill with its whitewashed walls and bell tower. The façade had three windows to the sky above, then four arches with the symbols of Catholic worship below, and at the bottom were windows, shaped like giant stars looking into the chapel and the figure of Christ at the altar.

Bella immediately noticed how tight the security was at the resort. The guest list was short but with some of the most important people in Mexico. This was an important day. The fifteen leaders of the Cartel Alliance joined the wedding party, Mitch and Bella, and an assembly of business leaders, community leaders, and politicians from both Mexico and Colombia. This was as symbolic as the nature of the event, marrying two people but also the relationships forged to create one of the most powerful alliances ever in Central and South America.

The chapel was lit up with tea lights and candles as sunset was considering closing its account for the day on the Baja Peninsula.

The ceremony would be brief, and the teachings would be of unity, community, alliance—teachings from the Bible carefully applied to this new world. The choir would sing their incantations, supported by the small orchestra, *Carmina Burana*, as composed by Carl Orff in 1936 but taken from the ancient twelfth-century parchment manuscripts discovered in the Benedictine monastery of Benediktbeuern in 1803.

This marriage had style. Style and meaning.

Bella watched the bride and the groom walk into the chapel together, a signal of unity and reform to the forty guests gathered and seated, reveling in the magical beauty of the chapel, the lights, the sunset, the music, and the aroma from the burning incense.

Bella sat with Mitch in the church, and as the ceremony unfolded, she quietly reached out and held her father's hand. They had been through a lot and both had their private thoughts. Bella's were about her mum, Nikita, Wills, and the rather handsome James Digby back in London. She squeezed Mitch's hand three times and felt the familiar three squeezes back, their own private code for *I love you*.

Bianca Blanca had planned everything, every last detail. It was a carefully thought-out, planned occasion. Afterward, they would eat and dance in the courtyard at the front of the chapel, as their ancestors would have done centuries before them. No airs and graces yet plenty of them as well, just not in a grand ballroom somewhere but underneath the stars, celebrating the world, their existence, and most importantly their alliance.

Bella and Mitch joined the throng and were equally in awe of the beauty of the evening, the setting, and the experience, and like the other guests, they felt a respectful, courteous admiration. The guest list was full of power, and that fueled the tension of the Cabo air.

Mitch had a quiet moment with Paulo Mancini. They embraced with big warm smiles like two brothers reunited, clearly with the deepest mutual respect.

Bella kept one eye on Dankov, who seemed to be keeping his pact between them, although she knew that ultimately, he was right. He had won. He had his power. Mitch didn't seek or desire what Dankov did, and the overspills of their rivalry just didn't make sense to either of them. Bad for business, as Dankov had put it. Bella agreed and saw the logic in letting sleeping dogs lie.

Dankov sat back, alone, Russian Standard in hand, Cuban cigar. He looked very pleased with his investment. Very pleased with himself indeed. *A grandmaster plays again.*

Bella noticed Mitch's phone buzz, and he stepped away to take the call. She watched him carefully, his face, his reaction; whatever it was, it clearly wasn't good.

Ripley Castle
Harrogate, North Yorkshire, United Kingdom
5:00 p.m.

Nestled in the woods by the deer reserve and the pheasant shooting grounds, a man watched as the wedding party arrived. He was dressed in his country outfit, not military, not camouflage, just the look of a sports hunter, common in these parts, and especially common on the Ripley Castle estate.

Tripod set up, telescopic sight. Just sitting, waiting, and watching his old friend Bob and his merry mates at the wedding party. *Yes, enjoy yourselves while you still can, my old, old friends from so long ago,* he thought. *From so long ago in the desert under a starlit sky.*

He watched as the day drew to a close and the lights in Ripley Castle started to make it look like some fairy-tale scene. He could see the guests at the wedding enjoying what he imagined to be their smoked salmon, caviar, and champagne.

Big Bad Bob had never seen his face all those years ago, on the rooftop of the compound. Only he had seen Bob's face, and it was etched in his memory forever. Neither of them had a clue who the other was when they first met in Malabo those years previously; the vagueness of memory and fifteen years of trying to erase it from his mind had seen to that.

Over time, with clues of the past, he had worked it out who Bob was or had been. He also worked out over time at least some of the crew that were with him that night. At least six of them were here tonight.

He spotted Silver Fox, Pearson, in his smart, immaculate suit, gray hair and piercing gray eyes, and for different reasons, he was glad he was here tonight. This enemy of his father was welcome to this party, his party.

The dark came down, and the night was clear and still, although a little chilly. He lit a Gitanes in the shelter of the woods, the continental aromas wafting through the air, neither the pheasant nor the deer apparently affected by the secondhand smoke.

He stared up at the sky, the stars and the constellations. He could spot the North Star, the Big and Little Dipper, the Great Bear. He had learned these things as a young boy, from a book one of his visiting uncles had left him. It reminded him of the song he used to listen to while stargazing, David Bowie's "Starman."

As the music in his head began to fade, someone on the raft on the lake before him was making final preparations for the show as the guests came out to the front of the castle, champagne flutes in hand.

As the firework display started in earnest and went on, he thought of the less grandiose fireworks in his hometown. He thought of his father, his mother, his younger sister. He thought of his tutor, his maids. He remembered his journey to Paris and his older sister and the shelter she had provided. He thought of his journey, the Legion, his brothers. He thought of the Russians kidnapping his sister and her children. He thought of the struggle. He thought of his revenge.

He now knew he was different and why his family was different and why they were killed in the night all those years ago. He now knew that there was a bigger purpose and a bigger calling for him. He would take care of this thing before him tonight, and then he would return to his rightful place as heir to his father and carry the fight in the next stage of the war. The holy war, the war of the Islamic State. This was his calling now. This was his duty. This was his future, but tonight was about revenge.

With great delight, the wedding guests whooped and hollered, screamed and cheered, the sound rippling over the lake to his vantage point in the woods opposite. After ten minutes, the wedding guests retired back into the castle to finish off their evening with whiskys and brandies and ports.

He pulled out a mobile cell phone, flipped it open, and opened the line as he watched the wedding party oblivious, having fun, drinking and dancing on their day of celebration.

He pressed the send button and the signal went to the multiple detonators located on the ground floor of the castle. He watched the fizzle, then the ripple of explosion and the fireball as the windows were blown out of their portals, splintering millions of shards of glass over the gravel apron at the front, where moments before they had been watching the fireworks.

The initial thunder and rawness of the blasts were followed by fire as the building recovered from its shakes, and the devastation was all that remained.

He closed the phone, packed up his tripod and gear, and turned one more time to witness the devastation before him.

"Allahu Akbar!" *God is most great* were his final words before he left into the darkness of the night.

27
AFTERSHOCK

Four Months Later
Langley, Virginia, United States
9:00 a.m.

BELLA WOKE UP IN HER apartment. It was Sunday, a day off—not that she really had days off, but usually on Sundays other people were off, so nothing came up, especially as it was the Sunday before Christmas. The sun was out in the blue sky, a crisp winter morning. Her Alexa Echo was playing Frank Sinatra Christmas songs, and Wills would be coming for breakfast in half an hour.

She had already been for her morning run—her usual seven miles, an almost daily habit, although as of late she had slacked. She found it hard to keep her routine when traveling, especially with the type of travel she did.

This would be her first Christmas in Washington. No Mitch, no mother, no cousins in California this year. After all, she was now a fully-fledged Central Intelligence Agency operative and by nature fully independent of all that. Or that was how it was supposed to be, but she had a heavy heart, as she missed her mum and dad, their walks on Blackie's Pasture, breakfasts at her favorite spots, playing chess and poker with her father, catching up on the latest Tiburon gossip with her mother, and the traditional roast meal with Yorkshire puddings.

This year, it was just going to be her and Wills. They had booked a table at the Willard, Washington's own Grand Dame with its marble and antiquities, with its honor and tradition, and with its Christmas Day buffet being one of the best in the city.

Bella had prepared their breakfast, kedgeree, one of Mitch's favorites but her own interpretation: Carnaroli rice, the king of risotto; Scottish smoked haddock; boiled eggs; and a touch of curry powder and sultanas, washed down with a bottle of Prosecco.

"Why not?" she said to herself. "Why the hell not!" She made a toast to herself and raised her glass. "It's Christmas after all."

Wills would be arriving soon. They would have breakfast and go shopping on Christmas Eve, enjoying the sounds of the season and kids laughing, families having fun, husbands last-minute shopping for wives, boyfriends shopping for girlfriends, and in her case, couples, together, sharing the moment.

It was a big day. She and Wills had had dinner the week before, and they had discussed the big question, and rather than some surprise on one knee affair, they would do it together. Bella didn't like surprises.

They would stop by Boone & Sons, famous for their diamonds, and stroll around.

Today was going to be a good day; she had convinced herself of that.

It was a big leap for Bella.

The last year had been interesting to say the least. The landscape of the world had changed, although the subtleties were not overtly obvious to the world. With information coming out through the press on a piecemeal basis, it was hard to put the puzzle pieces together to see the full picture and realize the connectivity and the weight of these events.

The coup in Equatorial Guinea fell into the noise of several other issues grabbing the attention of the press: China–US trade tensions, the South China Sea, US–North Korea denuclearization, Venezuela and Maduro hanging on to power, Russia flexing their military prowess around Europe and their energy superiority, Crimea and ongoing wrangling, Burma, allegations of Chinese concentration camps, the whole furor in Europe, and of course the Brexit issue.

In other words, in this day of free information and so much of it, the principles of maskirovka were far easier to apply.

President Trump seemed to have adopted similar practices. The news of a celebrity divorce, or an Oscar-winning nomination, the Super Bowl halftime show, Me Too accusations, and the weather were all candidates for masking over some of the real issues—some of the very serious issues.

Even climate change bore the brunt with the disbelievers' message, getting into the mainstream and the denial that the planet was changing. Affairs with glamour girls and porn stars got lost in the noise too. The assassination of Mandito in a domestic gas explosion didn't even make it to the news, nor did the Cartel Alliance or their alliance with Dankov, the Russians, and the Kremlin.

That would never make it to the press and public awareness.

Bella remembered the wedding at the Palmilla and couldn't help but admire the beauty of what Bianca Blanca had created—simple yet elegant, understated yet important, curated but not forced. That was the sort of wedding that Bella would want, maybe, maybe someday. She paused and took another slug of her sparkling wine.

She painfully remembered the call at the Palmilla to her father's phone and the devastation at Bob's wedding. She remembered the sadness, the funerals, the anger.

"Just because you have a ring on your finger doesn't mean that marriage is inevitable, right?" she asked herself.

What was she so fearful of? She didn't have an answer to that. Losing her independence? Probably. Stopping what she was doing? Maybe. The thought of having kids and how that would change her? Definitely. She knew that kids were high up on Wills's agenda.

But also, what about James Digby?

She paused again, holding the glass, as if about to sip, thought again, then took a sip, very slowly, looking off into the distance, a million miles away from the present.

One thing she knew she had to address was her relationship with violence. She, in a very strange way, enjoyed it. She knew that wasn't right, and she had to fix that. Somehow. She thought about Chip's offer of counselling and then quickly moved on from the thought.

Was it because of her father's teachings? She didn't think so. Could it be true that it was part of her blood? Her Scottish blood? Maybe so after all.

One true foot in front of the other. Bravely and truly. Boldly and rightly. Jock of the Park, William Wallace, Robert the Bruce. These were her ancestors, her countrymen. Could it be that her actions today were being influenced by those of the past?

Back to the present and the task in hand. Ironically, she was admiring her very Scottish creation before her as she took a quick spoonful of the rice and fish dish.

"Perfect." She gave a satisfied smile. Her cell phone vibrated, and she expected it to be Wills. Instead it was DAD. It was Chip Brown III, her friend and her boss at the agency.

"Hey, Chip, how's it going? Wishing me happy Christmas?"

"Hey, Bella. Happy Christmas," he said, full of sarcasm.

"Right back at you," Bella said. "What's going on?"

"Bella, we have an issue." Bella turned down Frank Sinatra singing one of his dulcet tunes so she could listen to every word. It must have been important for Chip to call. It was Christmas after all.

"Dankov promised to leave your father alone, which was all well and good. But the bomb in Ripley wasn't Dankov or his people, and it wasn't just some random act. It was some sort of revenge for an operation your father was involved in many, many years ago. Sixteen men were on that mission.

Thanks to the bomb and some other strange incidents, only five are now left, and Mitch is one of them."

Chip paused, and Bella said, "What operation?"

Chip said, "Bikini Bravo."

The words weighed on her like a suit of lead. Bella knew exactly what the mission Bikini Bravo was; she didn't need to ask any further questions, including who was responsible.

"We believe that there is a new head of ISIS, and he is getting revenge for the death of his parents and younger sister—from the Special Operations raid in Algeria."

"How imminent is the threat?" asked Bella.

"Imminent and very real. We have tracked several known operatives on the move and heading Mitch's way. This isn't just terrorism, Bella. This is terrorists with a name on their gun, and Mitch's name is on there in fucking neon lights."

"Who is it that has the vendetta?" asked Bella.

"His name is Hamza Malik."

Bella went white as a sheet as her skin went cold and the hairs on the back of her neck tingled from the chilling news. "Fuck. Okay. I'm on my way."

She hung up the phone, waited for Wills to arrive, and over the kedgeree told him that their shopping trip and Christmas lunch had been canceled. Something important had come up, and she was heading to Hereford, England, that evening.

Wills just looked at her and smiled. She saw that the smile was forced and that he felt both frustrated, sad, and maybe a little helpless. "I'm sorry," she said, her voice gentle and full of compassion. "My father is in danger. I have to be part of eliminating that danger. You can understand that, right? Given what I do for a living?"

Wills nodded and let out a big sigh. "Yeah, I get it, Bella. It's just that I'm disappointed. Very disappointed."

Bella felt a moment of annoyance. He seemed clingy sometimes. Too needy. Then the emotion left her. "I know you are," she said.

They said their goodbyes. Wills left. She wondered if they really did have a future together, one bright enough to consider marriage. *Oh, well,* she thought, *plenty of time now to give it more consideration.*

Bella went to her bedroom to pack her bag, and as she did, she flicked on the TV news.

London: ACC TV News: Equatorial Guinea President Dead

"Equatorial Guinea's former president was found dead in his London apartment over the weekend. The Metropolitan Police have yet to confirm the cause of death. Since the coup and his move to London, he has not been seen in public, keeping a very low profile. The news of his death is a shock. More to come as this story unfolds.

"Stuart Morris, ACC TV News. Good night."

EPILOGUE

AFTER THE DUST HAD SETTLED and the extent of what had just taken place over recent weeks became visible, the world witnessed one of the first land grabs of its type.

A complexity of Machiavellian proportions had spanned each side of the track, on the one side the legitimate intentions of the Russian Federation to extend its reach and influence—but the unorthodox nature of a partnership with the Russian Mafia and, in turn, an unlikely partnership with the drug cartels and partly funded by six criminal oil executives from a third-world country in Africa.

The people of Equatorial Guinea were all but worshipping Russia for its peaceful intervention from a credible force of unknown origin, the removal of their corrupt former president, and installation of the new.

The people of the Russian Federation were behind their leader as a new world leader—a leader to take them to their past glories and pride and away from the shame of the Soviet collapse.

Bianca Blanca, away from the eyes of the press and the public eye, had miraculously unified the cartels. They were working together, collaborating, self-governing under the banner of the historic charter that she had not only put together but had managed to get them all to sign and remain true to.

The mysteries around political meddling still existed, and the forces that be reveled in the speculation of their involvement in the US presidential elections, Brexit, and the wrangling of support, often united against the Western world, especially the United States.

Efforts were made to destabilize and undermine the US democracy, the greatest democracy in the world, and create uncertainty around the fabric of the United Kingdom, to potentially break apart, or at least exit Europe under Brexit, which could potentially break up the European Union itself. It was all part of a bigger strategy, but for whose material gain?

The world just watched. It had no choice. The game of chess was played by a grandmaster, and the opponent lost before even knowing that the game had started.

Maskirovka. Are you ready for the truth?

ABOUT THE AUTHOR

WILLY MITCHELL WAS BORN IN Glasgow, Scotland. He spent a lot of time in bars as a kid growing up and then in his youth and into adulthood. He always appreciated the stories—some true, some imagined, and some delusional. But these stories are true. Willy Mitchell was there!

A shipyard worker, he headed down from Scotland with his family to work in the steel mills of Yorkshire. He retired and turned to writing some of the tales that he had listened to over all those years, focusing on bringing those stories to life.

Operation Argus

Operation Argus is fast paced, thoughtful, and personal—an insightful story that touches the mind and the heart and creates a sense of intrigue in search of the truth.

While sitting in the Rhu Inn in Scotland one wintry night, Willy Mitchell stumbled across a group of men in civilian clothes, full of adrenaline, like a group of performers coming off a stage, wherever that stage had been that night.

To the watchful eye, it was clear that these men were no civilians. They were close-knit, bantering, and drinking beer yet completely alert as each of them checked him out. They looked at his eyes and into his soul. Willy Mitchell would learn in time that this group was referred to as call sign Bravo2Zero.

Operation Argus is a fictional story based around true events as five former, and one serving, Special Air Service soldiers converge on San Francisco for a funeral of their good friend to find his apparent heart attack is not as it seems. A similar concoction of Polonium-210 was used to assassinate Litvinenko in London years previously.

Bikini Bravo

Bikini Bravo continues to follow the adventures of Mitch, his daughter, Bella, and the team of Mac, Bob, and Sam as they uncover what seems an unthinkably complex web of unlikely collaborators for a seemingly obvious common good—power, greed, and money.

Many years ago, Mitchell stumbled across a bar in Malindi, Kenya, West Africa, and overheard the makings of a coup, the Wonga Coup in an oil-rich nation of West Africa. Could it be true that a similar plan was being hatched today?

Lord Beecham put together the pieces of the puzzle and concluded that the Russians along with the Mexican drug cartels and a power-hungry group of Equatorial Guineans put together an ingenious plot to take over Africa's sixth-largest oil-producing nation. It was the Russians' attempt to win influence in Africa, the cartels' desire for turning dirty money into good, and the Africans' desire to win power and influence.

Bikini Bravo is another book of fiction by Mitchell that masterfully flirts with fiction and real-life events spanning the globe and touching on some real global political issues.

Mitch's daughter, Bella, is the emerging hero in this, the second book of the Argus series.

Cold Courage

Cold Courage starts with Willy Mitchell's grandfather meeting with Harry McNish in Wellington, New Zealand, in 1929. In exchange for a hot meal and a pint or two, McNish told his story of the *Endurance* and the Imperial Trans-Antarctic Expedition of 1914.

According to legend, in 1913, Sir Ernest Shackleton posted a classified advertisement in the *London Times*: "Men Wanted: For hazardous journey, small wages, bitter cold, long months of complete darkness, constant danger, safe return doubtful. Honor and recognition in case of success." According to Shackleton, that advert attracted over five thousand applicants, surely a sign of the times.

Following the assassination of Archduke Ferdinand earlier that year, at the beginning of August, the First World War was being declared across Europe, and with the blessing of the king and the approval to proceed from the first sea lord, the *Endurance* set sail from Plymouth, England, on its way to Buenos Aires, Argentina, to meet with the entire twenty-eight-man crew and sail south.

Shackleton was keen to win back the polar exploration crown for the empire and be the first to transit across the Antarctic from one side to the other.

The *Endurance* and her sister ship, the *Aurora*, both suffered defeat, resulting in thirty-seven of Shackleton's men being stranded at opposite ends of the continent, cold, hungry, and fighting Mother Nature herself for survival.

This is a tale of the great age of exploration and the extraordinary journey that these men endured not only in Antarctica but upon their return to England amid the Great War.

This is the story of the *Endurance*, the Imperial Trans-Antarctic Expedition of 1914, and all that was happening in those extraordinary times.

Printed in the United States
By Bookmasters